I ooze out of the cab. I hop from shadow to shadow, my pistol handy, my gaze spinning like a top. I creep through the dank, gloomy canyon where piles of ordure fester and rats chitter over a dead dog that the carrion kids have missed. Every so often I put my foot down in a pool of sewage. It runs in at the lace holes. If I'm not sick in the next ten yards it's because I haven't had enough to eat.

I emerge into daylight. A few hundred yards away four towers, in a line, look as though they're about to set off on a march, but don't know which way to head. A fire smoulders, the smoke of old mattresses sniffs across the ground like a chimeric cat. Somebody moves, a distance away, disappears. Hard to believe this is still London.

Centre stage, thirty yards away, a middle-aged Negro, sobbing. Well he might. The poor sod has just been crucified.

TRAUMA 2020: BOOK 2

The Crucifixion Squad

Peter Beere

ARROW BOOKS

Arrow Books Limited
17–21 Conway Street, London W1P 6JD

An imprint of the Hutchinson Publishing Group

London Melbourne Sydney Auckland
Johannesburg and agencies throughout
the world

First published by Arrow 1984

Set in A.M. Compset by
Photobooks (Bristol) Ltd

Made and printed in Great Britain
by Anchor Brendon Limited, Tiptree, Essex

ISBN 0 09 934770 9

BOOK ONE

ONE

Would you mind not breathing into my face you bloody homo! I give one of my really heavy sighs, just to show the guy how really tolerant I am, and struggle up from the pit. I watch his teeth glint. How can anyone have teeth that glow in the dark? It doesn't make sense. Gorblimey, I rub my eyes. What time is it? Must be the middle of the bloody night, everyone's asleep.

What is the bloke after now? Why doesn't he go and breathe in someone else's goddamn face? God I'm knackered. 'Waddyerwant David, it's the middle of the fucking night.'

He shuffles nearer. If he gets any closer I'll be eating him. 'Beekay – you know you were talking about going to America – well we'd like to come, me and Ron –'

'Ron? Who the hell is Ron?'

'My boyfriend. You know, I was telling you about him.'

'Oh yeah.' I can't remember.

'Anyway – we thought, we'd like to come. If that's okay.'

Okay? You must be out of your flaming mind! I shake my head to clear some of the fuzz that my brain sleeps in. 'David, what are you talking about? How the hell can we go to America, we're inside a bloody prison! I mean it's all right for you, you only work here; you can just walk out the bloody place! I'm a flaming

7

con! By the time they let me out the States'll be off the bloody map!' I'm not sure what I meant by that, but it sounded pretty emphatic.

God, this crazy swish! I mean, he's a likeable enough guy, but his brains must have been left behind with his short trousers. I don't know, other people have guards who just beat them up; I've got one who fancies me and lives with the goddamn cuckoos.

'You're being sent to London tomorrow.'

'Me? What for, I thought they'd finished with me?' I've already got thirty bloody years, what more do they want?

'I don't know. Maybe they dug up something new. It's always happening.'

Thanks a bunch David. This is just what I need to soothe me to sleep. What are they going to do now, shoot me?

Suddenly chilled – which isn't hard as it's bloody freezing in here – I realize they might just do that, if they've figured out it was me who killed that flic Fitzwilliam. God, I thought I'd got away with that one; don't tell me they've drawn my card again. I thought all I had to do was spend the rest of my life in the can; I didn't know I had to spend it all in the next couple of weeks. Holy bollocks!

'I had a sort of plan. I thought maybe we could make some kind of deal.'

'A plan? What kind of plan?'

'What kind of plan do you bloody think? A plan to get us out of here!'

'You don't need a bloody plan! You're a flaming guard!' What is this, a dream, or what?

David sighed. 'But I wouldn't be would I, if I had any flaming choice!'

8

'Why, what do you want to be?' Gorblimey, we're in a barrack hut full of four hundred desperate criminals, and we're having a career talk!

'I don't know. I don't want to do this for the rest of my life though.'

'Well quit.'

'I can't. You have to sign up for it, it's like the army. I either went in the infantry, or I came here.'

Yeah, that was like me. Only I came in through the other entrance. The one without a handle. I looked around to see if anyone was listening to us. Lacking infra red vision was a disadvantage, I couldn't see a bloody thing. It was blacker than a cave bat's bedroom. 'What's the deal?' I hissed.

'Well –' I sensed him shrug – 'I get you out, you help me get Ron out – we all go to the States.'

'Get Ron out? What is he, in a bucket of cement or what?' I didn't like the sound of this.

'He's in Wandsworth B. He used to do a bit of pushing. He got six years.'

Oh great! That's how I got in here in the first place, trying to spring someone! Forget it David.

But on the other hand – killing coppers is a capital offence. If I threw over this chance, how many more were there likely to be? And what's to stop me just lying to the guy, and doing a split? Yeah, all right, I know, conscience – don't remind me. Don't think you can rely on it for ever though, sooner or later I'll get the better of it. Maybe this is the time.

David was obviously a bit worried by my silence. 'I think we could do it Beekay. I mean, you've had experience of that kind of thing – and I'm pretty good with guns. . . .' Good with guns! What does he think we're going to do – storm the bloody place?

'He's not in the prison all the time. Mostly he's out on workparties, I thought that's when you could get him. He's a nice guy. You'd like him.'

Yeah, I've heard that before. 'David – what sort of plan have you got?' I'm not sure David's all there really. I mean, for a start his choice of con leaves a lot to be desired! I'm about as much use at this blood-and-guts stuff as a cow at laying eggs.

But having tasted eighteen months of prison life, I can see that desperation has its attractions.

'Well, there's three vans going in the morning, and you'll be in the last one with Sharky and Lafferty. I'll do a swap with Lafferty, cos he gets travel sick, and when we get to a good spot I'll clobber Sharky and we'll take off.'

Oh yeah, bloody simple! There's only about two hundred things can go wrong! Two hundred – count them. I don't trust simple plans. If it's that easy, why doesn't everyone do it? It was like this when I did sums at school; if they seemed easy, I always assumed I'd got them wrong. And I usually had.

'What do you say? Do you want to give it a try?'

Wait a minute, wait a minute, let me think. 'Are we taking off in the van, or what?'

'Yeah. You'll have to drive, I don't know how.'

'I'll be chained up in the back won't I?'

'Yeah. I'll have to figure that one out; we don't keep the keys here, they're all at the other end.'

There's a weak spot for a bloody start! And something else was bothering me. 'Why me?'

'I don't know. You just seem, all right really.'

Oh, just the quality we need to risk our lives for. They'll probably put that on our tombstones. 'Seemed all right, really.' This whole thing stinks. Maybe I am

10

having a dream after all, I dream a lot of weird things these days.

'Don't you fancy it?'

'What do you think? Would you fancy it?' The guy lying next to me rolled over and nearly ripped my goddamn arm off. We're handcuffed together.

'It's better than thirty years on the Ditch.'

He's right. I tugged my arm back. Cancer of the bollocks is better than thirty years on the Canal. I've been on it for ten months now – in one of the mobile prisons up Watford way – and it's done everything but turn me inside out.

What a great choice, hey? I can have three decades on the Canal – if my body holds out that long, which I doubt – or I can jump off the scaffold, or I can take a chance on this crazy swish who cleans his teeth with Old Spice. The trouble is, although the last one looks the best bet, I have to actually *do* something. With the other two I can just be myself and drift along, hoping something will turn up. The famous ostrich approach. A technique I've been practising for many years.

But would you rather be an ostrich or a dodo? God, I wish I had a crystal ball. It'd probably shatter in this bloody weather. It's the coldest February since the last bloody one. Oh God, I don't know, what should I do? I'll go! No I won't. Yes I will. 'I'll go!'

'Okay.' David disappeared, before I had a chance to say anything else. Before I had a chance to change my mind. Maybe he knows me better than I think.

TWO

Morning came and the rain was hammering down. Pitter patter pitter patter through the window panes. Most of which have gone on vacation.

I stood in a doorway, with a sheet of polythene over my head to keep the rain off, and watched the crew shuffle off to work. They didn't say a word, only their chains clanked. They were like a bunch of vagrant spooks. They didn't look happy. Nobody looks happy any more. Even I look miserable, and you know what a cheery guy I am.

I watched them shamble into the obscuring rain until they vanished. Good riddance! Piss off! I hope that's the last I have to do with any of you! Ten months I've been slaving here, and I didn't know any of them. Not that I'd bloody want to, they're a bunch of flaming psychos.

I rubbed my wrist where the chain had been removed. It was one long abscess where the metal had chafed and the grit had been ground into the skin. I stopped rubbing, it was bloody agony. God, I hope they never send me to work on the Canal again.

The flappy polythene flapped and the hours trudged by. It's always like this. My fingers turned blue, then white, then threatened to drop off altogether. The wind shifted round so that it could fire the rain under the polythene, right into my face. But I couldn't turn around, it's 'not allowed'. Somewhere in the prison handbook there's a rule that says you're not allowed to

12

face the wall. Probably in case you get sexually aroused by the sight of a brick.

Eventually the goddamn vans rolled up. Must have taken a detour through bloody Birmingham. Then we had to wait while everyone went in for a cup of tea and said 'Gee, great, you're only seven hours late!'

The vans sat looking at us. And we stood stupidly, staring back at them. There were ten of us. The rain streamed down. The vans steamed and clucked. The guy standing next to me pitched forward into the mud, unconscious. I told them he wasn't well. Ah, what the hell.

Then two rackety old motorbikes came slushing up. Additional escort. Christ, this idea of David's looks more and more suspect all the time. We haven't got a cat in hell's chance.

Vroom! Vroom! We started up, with the blast from the lousy exhaust going right up my back passage. There should have been a ledge to sit on, but it had rusted away and we just had to squat down and make out as best we could. We would have sat down but the floor was wet. With the slops from other people's bladders.

We moved off and I was happy as a sandboy. That's bitter sarcasm by the way; in reality I was about as low as a guinea pig's kneecaps. Spirits so low you couldn't find a rope long enough.

Had a lot to worry about too. I hadn't seen David all day, I didn't know what the hell was going on. I didn't know whether he'd managed the swap, or anything. And what was I supposed to do, kick up a din, or what?

I crouched in the corner like a sick owl, clicking

13

through the links of my chain like they were worry beads. The two joes opposite told me to button it, so I did. You know me, always eager to please. Always scared I'm about to get smashed.

The van bumped along. I stared at my boots. I was starting to feel sick. Well, to be honest, if we didn't stop soon I'd be puking up in all directions.

Almost at once we stopped. It's creepy that kind of thing, I hate coincidences. It was also scary as hell. It didn't sound like we were there yet – like there were no metal gates slamming shut, no savage dogs tearing at their chains. So maybe David was making his move. God, what's going to happen now? What about all those bloody guns that they're all carrying? Oh Christ, I wish I'd been born a girl. I'd probably be a wife and mother now. I wish . . .

Footsteps. The wishes have all run out. One of the back doors opens, a crowd of daylight bundles in, poking us all in the eyes. I squint.

Framed in the dazzlement are a couple of angels. A little fat one and a tall elegant one. The fat one is the driver, Sharky – because he has a skin wart on the top of his head that looks like a dorsal fin – and he looks pretty lachrymose. I guess that's understandable, even discounting the skin wart, which is pretty disgusting. The tall one, the one pressing a pistol into the back of Sharky's neck, is David.

'You okay in there?'

I nodded. I was a bit too nervous to speak. I was damn nearly too nervous to breathe, there was a great clamping pain in my chest. But I nodded again just to show myself I could. In fact once I'd started I could hardly bloody stop, my neck went into a kind of spasm.

David handed Sharky a pickaxe. 'Get him out of there.' He glanced up and over the roof of the van. 'Shit, here comes one of the bikes,' he muttered.

Sharky made a half-hearted attempt to prise the chain out of the floor. Then everything went quiet as a motorbike glided to a halt beside the van. The guy killed his motor. I heard a muffled question. Probably asking the latest Stock Market moves. I heard his machine creak as he shifted his weight.

David slammed the door open, right into the bike. He gave it a kick for good measure, lammed the motor-cyclist in the face with his boot. The guy should have kept his visor down, his nose was no protection at all. It just burst into floods of crimson tears.

Sharky swung into action with all the desperate ponderosity of the truly fat man. Turned on David's exposed back with his pick held high. I tried to shout a warning.

But I needn't have bothered. David sidestepped, turned, sent a cluster of pneumatic bullets splatting into the fat man's puss. Jesus Christ, I didn't know a gun could fire that fast. I buried myself as bits of nose and cartilage sprayed through the air and a lump of brain landed hot on my hand. Blood dripped off the doors like the rain of hell. Sharky's last cup of tea started coming out of his mouth, along with a lot of other stuff.

David turned to the rider, groaning on the ground, kicked him hard in the back of the neck. He went quiet then.

That wasn't the end of it though. One of the bullets that smashed through Sharky's skull ricocheted off the roof of the van and hit one of the guys opposite me in the eye. Fancy being shot by a second-hand bullet. He started shrieking, rolling about gobbing blood and yuk, and there was an almighty bollocks for a couple of minutes until I got my boot in his face to shut him up. Then he went quiet too.

But the other guy took sides and leapt on me. Must have been his wife or something. The goddamn chain was just long enough to allow him to beat the crap out of me. I yelled for help. He'd just got his fingers inside my nose, about to rip it off, when a shot from David's pistol took his bloody ear off. Thank God he's on my side. I'm getting to like the guy more all the time. My assailant fell away bellowing. Let that be a lesson to you! I kicked him as well.

David handed me the pickaxe. I tried to ignore the blood on the handle. 'Where did this come from?'

'I said I was lifting it for my brother's allotment. Best get a move on Beekay, the other vans'll be coming to look for us in a minute.'

I wedged the point of the axe into the staple in the floor and heaved like the buggery. Nothing. I could have been trying to split an atom. I gave up, panting. David took it, gave a little tug and half the goddamn floor ripped out. 'You were pulling it the wrong way.' I just grunted. I hate humiliating myself. I started gathering up the chain.

David chucked a look over the roof of the van. 'They're coming.' He passed me Sharky's pistol and picked a shotgun up from the roof.

'Stuff that,' I said. 'Let's sod off.' What's the point of standing still when you've still got a chance to run?

We scampered round to the front and dived in. I bundled all the chain and bits of metal after me. 'Where are the frigging keys?'

'They must be in his pocket.'

'Well go and get them for chrissake! Don't just

16

bloody sit there!' I felt terror blasting up my guts. 'Give me the gun!' Easy Beak, don't lose control!

While David darted out I leaned out of the window and blasted off at the nearer of the two approaching vans. Gorblimey, what a bloody noise! Have you ever fired a shotgun? Makes all your teeth numb. And it nearly broke my bloody shoulder. Not only that, the barrel must be bent. I blew out someone's front window. But it scared the van, it swung hard away, crunched through a tatty privet hedge into someone's empty garden. There'll be letters to the council about this, I'll bet.

We were in a wide street, lined with skinny trees, still in their winter clothes. Semi-detached bay windows bellied out, stumpy rose bushes bristled in the cold wind, old election stickers flapped, daubed slogans dripped. Like dull, I guess you'd call it. A dead black cat was hanging from a lampstandard, sodden and limp. Sometimes even nine lives aren't enough.

A couple of bozos were dumbstruck, their tongues were taking the air. A little girl was pointing, a finger up her nose and a wonky blue hat sliding down over one eye. The backside of the frightened van stuck crudely out of the privet hedge, the frantic wheels burrowing holes in the soft grey earth. The driver must have passed out. Either that or the accelerator had a mind of its own. Probably more than the driver has.

The second van swung across the road to bar the way. It looked pretty tough. I didn't like the look of it at all.

I started hollering. David appeared and stuck the keys in my hand. I jammed them into the slot. The van started leapfrogging. Well it might, it was still in bloody gear. I stamped on the clutch. I pulled what I

17

thought was the handbrake and the fucking bonnet bounced up.

These vans are bloody useless! I couldn't see out the back, the wing mirror had snapped off and the flaming window wouldn't wind down. I crunched into reverse, hung out of the door like a bloody drunk. Wallop! We hit a frigging tree! Sod this for a bloody lark! Fighting down my panic I flung us forward. Broom!!

'Watch that kid on the bike!'

I swung round hard but I still hit him. Shit. He'd have probably fallen off anyway, I just gave him a little nudge. Look, he's getting up now. Anyway it wasn't a kid, it was a bloody dwarf. 'It's not a kid, it's a bloody dwarf!' I didn't know they made motorbikes that small. You don't see a lot of dwarfs . . .

'Look out!'

Jesus Christ! I forgot about the other motorcyclist. The van slewed wildly and we still managed to hit him. He landed on the bonnet, clinging on to the bloody windscreen like a nightmare! Can't see a flaming – *bang*!! David fired the bloody shotgun through the window! Oh fucking brilliant David, now we can't see anything! He started knocking out the mosaic of shattered glass.

The van jumped over the kerb, burst into somebody's front garden. I was tussling madly with the wheel and just managed to avoid their front-door, smashing through a fence into next door's garden. I put my foot down. The family cat shot up the front wall on to the roof.

I started demolishing more garden fences. David hung out of the window, loosing off bullets in all directions. Jesus Christ, how do you get out of second gear on this thing?

We took a broadside from the van in the road. But they were too slow, hit the van in the midriff and we were in the head. A lot of wailing came from the back though. Someone had caught a gutful.

I swung back on to the road. Just in time, someone's concrete fountain was squaring up for a showdown. Just missed a tree. Found out all the noise was because I was trying to shove it into first gear.

'They're coming after us!'

The van snarled forward. I was panting like a threatened virgin, sweat was pouring into my eyes. Head down, I gunned us down the street. Let's see you catch this one baby!

Missed the corner though. We swung round crazily, tyres screaming with terror. The world went into a demented spin. Ended up in a launderette. Where the hell did that come from? The engine shrieked, died with a great hiss, its radiator battered senseless by a dry-cleaning machine. We sat for a moment, stunned. I wiped my nose on my sleeve.

Now what? What the hell else can go wrong? Need an idea quick. Nothing.

Can't just sit here.

'We'd better start running, Beekay.'

You said it man. We tumbled out. I jammed the pistol in my belt, bundled up my chain. David blew the lock off the back door, we kicked it open, legged off down an alley.

It was about time we had some good luck. But Fate didn't agree. Ran slap into a twelve-foot bloody fence full of barbed wire, pointed railings, electric rayguns the lot. Son of a goddam bitch! We started climbing. Halfway up my chains got the better of me and I slipped off. Being an adept at the art of landing like a pillock, I contrived to break my fall with my chin. My teeth met in the middle of my tongue. My mouth foamed with blood.

'Are you all right?'

All right? I'm fucking senseless! I staggered up stunned, while David perched precariously on the top to wait for me. I thrashed about like an angry gorilla but I couldn't get the goddamn chain free. It was hooked over one of the railings. David's nerve snapped and he started yelling at me. I spat out mouthfuls of blood like a vomiting vampire.

God dammit! Why is everything going wrong? I yanked at the chain in a great impression of a hysterical madman. 'Will you come off for chrissake, you bloody . . . !' A gun boomed. I looked around. The third van had found us out.

I looked up at David but he'd vanished. I thought for a moment he'd been shot, but he'd just done a bunk. I threw myself to the ground, tried to get the pistol out without blowing my goddamn balls away. God, this isn't one of my better days.

I couldn't get the gun out. And a glance upwards told me I was too late anyway. The two guards from the pursuit van had me cold; they were only a few yards away, hiding behind their shotguns. It was time for an act of reckless heroism, or abject surrender.

'Don't shoot! I give up!' I cried.

They mustn't have heard me. Or maybe they did. Either way, one of them fired; maybe to scare me, maybe to bolster himself. Maybe he just had a twitch. He hit the alley floor about two feet in front of me.

It was like being walloped by a sack of nails. Lumps of grit spanked into my face like angry wasps. Everything inside my head slammed and went numb;

my eyes seemed to squeeze through cracks at the back of their sockets. I gasped.

If the guy wanted to frighten me he succeeded with a bloody vengeance. I thought he'd blown my bloody head off. I couldn't even see anything, all I could hear was this noise in my brain like a great tidal wave rushing about looking for an exit. Finally it went spilling out of my ears and I shook my head numbly. 'Fucking hell,' I muttered. I started choking.

But while the two lawmen concentrated on reducing me to a quivering wreck, the rest of my team materialized on a fire escape about thirty yards away and opened up with awesome precision.

He used to win medals for shooting, did David. He's a bastard with a gun. He could shoot your bloody eyelashes off. He could shoot the goddamn plaque off your teeth.

He shot the first gazebo through the eye. That's what he's like; me, I'm happy if I get a bullet in the same *street* as the target; David picks off bits of a target.

I heard the splat! as the bullet smacked through the guy's skull. I thought maybe he'd scream, or leap about or something. But he didn't, he just went straight down like an empty overcoat without a bloody sound, a spurt of blood rushing on ahead to show him the way. And then his brain made a last desperate effort to do something constructive; but all it managed was to open up his bowels in a sudden heave.

The other guy gurgled for a minute, then bolted. And I didn't blame him, they don't pay them to get shot to pieces. But he was too late. He'd only gone a dozen steps when the back of his head burst open and started spewing blood and egg-white all down his back. At least, that's what it looked like. He bounced off his face, and crawled along for about fifteen feet. But he was dead after five of them. No one told his fingers that though, they kept twitching and scrabbling for ages.

God, I don't like this kind of thing at all. I mean, I don't like people one little bit, as misanthropes go, I'm an expert. But being misanthropic's one thing – I mean, it's all kind of cerebral. Being involved with the slaughter of folk, even when your life is on the line, it's not something you can easily grow accustomed to. I think you have to be born to it. It makes my guts collide and freezes my voice.

David came back and helped me get the chain free. I couldn't say a word. We climbed over the fence, trotted off into the evening, looking for lots of things; a hacksaw, a bed, a bit of peace and quiet. Some obliteration. Brr. Shudders ran through me in regular waves. It's hard to hate people when they've just died gruesome deaths.

Look, there's that bloody dwarf again! What's he doing, following us? He's probably annoyed because I knocked him off his bike. There's always somebody getting in your bloody way.

THREE

Hit the quiets again, thank God. It's just as well, I can't take the rough stuff for long. In fact, I can't take it at all. Roll on old age, that's what I say. Put me in a rest home.

Shee, so what's happening now? Not a lot. Life goes on.

Do you know how many bones there are in the human body? No, neither do I. But I thought I'd broken every one of them when I fell downstairs this morning. Fucking kids. Tied a piece of bloody wire across didn't they? I'll poke their bloody eyes out if I catch them; I hate kids.

Anyway, we're just thinking about how to rescue the boyfriend, Ron. Whoever the hell he is. Why have I got to go and risk my neck for someone I don't even know? I don't understand life at all you know.

If I was a bastard, I'd just bugger off and leave him. I mean, I've got my own life to lead. I've got things of my own to do. I've got to find Harry and Rachel and Gay. At least two of whom, being the first two, are in the can somewhere, thanks to that bloody disaster at Leighton Buzzard. Half the damn prison got away and we got caught! And then we've got to get to America. That's not going to happen overnight you know. It needs planning, endeavour, organization – all those things I'm not much good at.

Actually, it might not be a bad thing if David and

Ron did team up with us. I mean, it's not enough to just have the money to pay the fare – assuming it's still in that hole in the ground and the worms haven't eaten it. You need to be pretty, well, hard, too. A lot of folk are only too anxious to rip you off and chew you up. A couple of extra blokes might not go amiss. Even if they do wear make-up.

Can you trust them though? Oh, I think so. David seems a nice enough bloke; you've got to trust somebody haven't you?

Shame about his clothes-sense though. I asked him to pick me up a couple of cheap shirts while he was out; the one I had on the Canal was falling to bits. Not to mention that it's got my prison number stamped all over it. So he came back with a yellow one with orange dots, and a turquoise lurex thing with little pink teddy bears. I thought it was a bloody rainbow walking through the door.

There is one consolation I suppose; we save on electricity. I glow in the dark.

So here we go, about to make the snatch, swinging into action with all the grace and precision of a well-oiled machine, I don't think. God, I don't fancy this at all. I wouldn't even want to *watch* this, never mind taking a starring role. Are you sure you need me David? Wouldn't you rather have someone with a few guts? I think I left mine in the bog this morning. Had a dose of bloody diarrhoea.

Gorblimey, I don't fancy this at all at all. I've already spent eighteen months in the slammer, ten of which were spent digging out that flaming Canal. All of a sudden I can see it looming up in front of me again. And this time they might remember the things they forgot to charge me with the last time. Like blowing up that copper.

What d'you say David, why don't we just sneak off home? He'll be out in six years, you'll be able to surprise him with a nice little log cabin in the Rockies. He doesn't listen. He's besotted. I wouldn't mind, but they're only *unofficially* engaged.

Anyway, I don't like it here at all. Cemeteries give me the bloody willies. I'd rather be queuing up to be circumcized than have to spend any time in a graveyard.

Too many flaming vampire movies, that's my trouble. Like, ordinarily, I don't believe in the great undead. Cos most of the time I'm not thinking about them. It's only when I start thinking about them that I get worried. And a graveyard doesn't half put that kind of thought in your mind! Creaking coffins and long white hands, shadows hopping from tombstone to tombstone. I don't like it. I don't like it at all.

This cemetery, which I'm looking at now, is worse than most. Mainly because they're digging it up. Little Ron, put away for several years for pushing stardust and heroin, and a man more suited to smoothing the fine hairs on the back of David's neck, is stacking coffins on the back of an old lorry, and cracking open tombs with a sledge.

I cross myself. It's at moments like this that my Catholic superstitions rise to the surface. I put the field glasses down and rub my eyes. Either these bloody things are steaming up all the time, or I'm going blind.

Gather close, I'll tell you what's going on. We're in west London. Very west, in fact, almost at the airport.

Which is now mostly an adventure playground and an army camp.

Got a great view from up here, splayed on a rooftop. Great for viewing, torture for my vertigo. That's what's wrong with my eyes; they're sweating.

Before us and below us is the cemetery. Beyond that, after a tangle of weeds and rubbish, runs the Grand Union Canal. The canal, being widened to come up to the standards of the much larger Canal of Winston Cooper's dreams (the former Home Secretary, remember?), is being broadened in the direction of the cemetery. In fact it will end up swallowing most of the graves, which is not a good idea, unless you like to have coffins chugging along the waterways of Britain. And even these days, there are people who might object. So the graveyard is being moved.

At least, that was the idea. But what is really happening, (I get all this info from the one-eyed woman in the caff round the corner) is that the coffins are being taken away to be burned, and the tombstones are being polished down and sold abroad. And they're not even being burnt at the crematorium, they're going to the council incinerator in Ealing! There's just no respect for the dead now you know. It's a good job this is a Protestant cemetery or I'd be really annoyed. I'm surprised they don't sell the bodies to a bloody restaurant.

So, all the tombstones are being stacked against one wall of this pillaged Golgotha and the coffins are being tossed on the back of a council lorry. Together with the plastic bags that have been filled with all the bits of those which have decomposed. Two old men, who look like they should have been buried themselves years ago, are employed shovelling them up.

This seems as good a time as any to make a grab for

26

Ron. There's a lot of coming and going. I wish we were.

Hell, I hope David's more confident than I am. I wouldn't touch it with somebody else's barge pole. Trouble comes to you easily enough; walking in to look for it is bloody ludicrous. Gives me the collywobbles. In fact if they wobble much more I'll be losing them.

We size up the distance from the empty flat on the fifth storey of a tower block to a copse of dead conifers just beyond the graveyard wall. 'Can you chuck that far?'

David shrugs. 'Well if I can't, you certainly bloody won't.'

He's right. We'd thrown a few rocks to compare our arms. Mine is bloody pathetic. No need for him to be so dismissive though, is there?

'I suppose we'd best get on with it then.' All the enthusiasm of a spotty kid on a blind date. All sorts of weird rumblings in my belly. Sometimes, I think my body's been invaded by flaming aliens.

We trudge up the stairs. Squeeze past a couple of kids burning the wings off bluebottles on one of the landings.

The door to the fifth-floor flat is open. Well, not open so much as gone completely. We enter cautiously, pick a way through all the crap to the back room.

While I unpack the bag David taps the rest of the glass out of the window. I lay out the pieces of his rifle, check the can. The place is full of rubbish. Bottles, johnnies, broken furniture, stinking newspapers. It smells like a sick dog's vomit. There's mould on the walls as deep as your thumb.

27

David knocks out the last frame of glass, fits his rifle together. I have a squint from the empty window. It's a clear day. Nearly noon. Gulls drifting against the blue like they're asleep. A wind blows across the February landscape. Children scream. Far below, someone on a bicycle gets a puncture; you can hear his imprecation from here.

In the cemetery, the workparty labours quietly. Little figures in their prison blues, they look like treasure-hunters. About thirty cons. Four warders. Kitted out with shotguns that look like they can bring down aircraft. If one of them hit you I doubt you'd know about it.

The cemetery looks like a blueprint for a necro-philiacs' holiday camp.

They have to employ prisoners on this kind of work now. Half of the real workers are away at the war, there's no money to pay the rest and the whole bloody country's falling apart. There's just no sanity to it. If they didn't have so many cons, the whole place would grind to a halt. It's only crawling now.

'Are you sure this thing will work?' asks David.

'It says so on the label.'

He frowns at the tin, tries to read the small print. I wouldn't bother, it's in Russian.

We'd been out to Leighton Buzzard on the bus and I'd dug up some of the stuff me and Harry had buried there. Two days it took us to get there; it's only up the bloody road. We had a couple of grand in cash, the last grenade and a canister of oblivion gas, which knocks people out.

A little girl appears at the inner doorway. 'What you doing?'

'Piss off.'

28

'It won't blow up will it?'

'Course it won't blow up,' I say. 'It blows up if you detonate it, or if you set fire to it. Just lobbing it won't do any harm.'

A little doubtful, David takes up a position in the middle of the room. 'You ready?'

I have a last look out of the window. The yard below is empty. Everyone in the cemetery is busy. I nod, chomp into a Mars Bar, step aside.

The idea is to get the can of gas into the graveyard so that it lays everybody cold. Then, in a couple of minutes when it's cleared, we go and collect Ron. The rifle's just in case. Daedalian really. Yeah, I know it's bloody stupid, but what else can you do? We couldn't just toss it over the wall, cos one of the guards is sitting on it. Anyway the wind might change direction. Not much point knocking everyone out if you're one of them.

David has a couple of practice swings. He has to throw it sideways. Bit awkward man. Finally he pulls off the ring-pull and lets it go.

Whizz! It clears the top of the window by about an inch, sails out like a yellow bird. We step forward to watch it fall.

Oh, lovely throw, look at that! Arcs gracefully across the wall, smack into the middle of the trees. And then there's an enormous goddam explosion. A dozen coffins fly through the air.

'Holy shite!'

That about sums it up David. My teeth stop chewing on the Mars Bar. My eyes gawk. God, it went off like a flaming atom bomb! Maybe we should have tried to read the label. Must have been the wrong can.

People start scurrying into the yard to see what's

29

going on. Then bodies start collapsing. The gas must have been blown all over the place.

'Half of London must have heard that!'

He's right. This isn't going to plan. I think rapidly. Come up with nothing.

'We'd better do something quick, Beak!'

I know, I know! What though? I thump my forehead. 'You'd better cover me. I'll go and get him.'

'What about the gas?'

'Er – it'll go in a minute. We'll hang on until people stop falling over. That should be okay.' I looked around, panicky. 'No good from here though, you might get cut off. We'd best go downstairs.'

We charged down the flights to the second floor, picked out a door, kicked it off its hinges. Doesn't half hurt your ankle that. The oldish couple inside started screaming as we burst in. 'Police!' I yelled. 'Police! Police! Move out of the way!'

They fell obediently to one side as we barged past. David knocked the pane out of the kitchen window. Sorry about this love. Still, it'll let some of the flies out. What do you feed them on, they're bloody monsters!

Down below one or two hombres were staggering about. The gas must be clearing, it's a breezy day. 'I'll go get him then. Anyone comes, just shoot them.' It's survival of the self now, no time for fancy stuff. David nods grimly. Other people look grim, me, I just look scared.

I ran downstairs, through the doors at the back, across the yard, scrambled over the red sandstone wall into the ravaged necropolis. It's horrible. There are opened graves and blasted corpses all over the place.

I find Ron, upside down in an empty grave. At least I think it's him, he doesn't look quite the same as in

David's photograph. Maybe it's all the mud. Or maybe it's because he's got no make-up on.

I drag him out. Hoist him up into a sad parody of a fireman's lift. I look more like a coalman. I stumble across the battered ground. At this point a bit of co-operation from Ron would be appreciated, he keeps trying to slide off head first. I have to grab him by the balls to keep him up there. It's a bloody good job he's unconscious.

I bundle him over the wall, crouch beside him, poke an inhaler up his nose, spurt a few spurts. He shakes his head, starts to come round.

'Hoi! Hoi! Is your name Ron? Hoi! Wake up!'

He wakes up, but in panic starts to thrash out. Nearly pokes my bloody eye out. 'For Christ's sake you stupid bugger, I'm trying to rescue you! Me and David!'

He's too groggy to understand. Either that or he's just plain stupid. 'Never mind. Come on.' I drag him up, lead him across the yard. I give David a wave. He meets us at the front of the building. Several people are looking at us curiously. I'm not surprised. David's rifle is sticking out of the top of his trousers and Ron keeps falling over.

We freeze to listen. Sirens.

Quickly men! We've got this motorcycle and sidecar thing for the getaway. What a bloody joke! Cost me a bleeding fortune and it's falling to bits. I get the thing started at about the four millionth attempt and we roar off, clattering and banging like a group of copulating robots. There's so much goodamn smoke coming out the thing looks to be on fire.

The sirens howl closer but it looks like we're going to miss them. We race through empty streets, bouncing over potholes and bricks. Deserted office blocks peer down at us. Once fancy walkways and flyovers threaten to collapse on top of us. Litter gusts into our faces. A few kids cheer. A few throw bricks. All these empty buildings. All this dying city.

This is only the second time I've been on a motorbike. I'm not doing too badly. We've only hit one cat, and that was blind anyway.

It's a good job we're not going far. Aside from the conspicuousness of it all, we could hardly get any petrol for the damn thing; I keep expecting it to pack up at any moment. The stuff we did get looked watered-down to me. It looked as though the pump had a kidney disease.

Big problem is we have to go everywhere in straight lines. I can't get the damn thing to turn. Every time I try to take a corner the machine just carries on going. We all have to get off and lift it into a new direction. That guy really ripped me off.

FOUR

So, we pulled it off and now little Ron shares this cheap, grubby apartment with the rest of us. That's me and David, and a load of silverfish and bugs and things. There are so many of them, they pull the blanket off you in the night.

He's a cute enough sort of bozo, in a moderate kind of way. Like, I'm not crazy about him, but I can stand him. He goes really bananas about going to America though. I have to keep calming him down. There's a long way to go yet, and not just in terms of miles.

Yeah, everyone wants to go to the States. The place might stink but it still smells better than this side of the water. At least they're not at war there. Well, not much. Only with each other.

Got to get there first though. No time to sit around listening to Ron squeal while he packs our suitcases for the hundredth time. I've got to get on. I wouldn't mind but we haven't got enough to fill a plastic bag never mind a bloody suitcase.

Trouble is, I've got no ideas at all on how to set about finding where Harry and Rachel are. I could walk into the Prison Department and ask, I suppose. But it might not be one of the wisest moves in the history of the world.

And Gay, I'm not sure what happened to her. I think she got away, but news was a bit scarce in Canterbury gaol, which is where I ended up. So I'm back to my usual position of banging my head against the bloody wall, seeking inspiration. If you've got any ideas, let me know quick.

There's one funny thing though, that I've half a mind to check up on. But I can't decide if it's worth the effort. I can't really see how it's connected with me. It's probably just a coincidence.

On the other hand, it is a funny sort of coincidence. Mind you, I suppose they all are. See, I always look through the personal ads. I've got a kind of obsession with them. The other week, it was last week in fact, there was a little one-liner in the evening rag. 'Beak, contact ma, Dwarfy.'

I thought, that's funny, that's my name, Beak. Honestly, I'm like lightning sometimes. An IQ that runs to a second digit. But I didn't think like too much about it. I mean, I don't know any Dwarfy, and my ma's in a little tin somewhere. Bloody dwarfs though. It's funny, isn't it, how they keep cropping up?

Anyway, the ad was there again last night. And I got to thinking about it, the way one does. Thought over all the dwarfs I know. That didn't take long, how many dwarfs does anybody know? Dwarfs, midgets – wondered on to the Seven Dwarfs. Flo Bright and the Seven Dwarfs, that was a famous sex case a little while back. Happy, Sleepy, Grumpy – Happy? Gay?

Gay? Nah, it couldn't be. Just a coincidence. Too bloody silly. It's like some espionage story.

And what about my old dam, polishing the knocker on the Pearly Gates with a pair of old underpants? How am I supposed to get in touch with her? Shout? I'm not going to a seance or anything like that. Brr, spooky man. It's all stupid. I'm probably just bored. My mind's starting to ramble. I blow my nose, find out too late

34

there's a big tear in my handkerchief. God Almighty. . . .

On the other hand – which must be about the third one I've moved on to – I suppose I could pay a visit to the crematorium, just to pay my respects.

Can't help shaking my head though. Bloody Dwarfy! I must be out of my mind. It's probably some cipher for perverts.

I'll take David along with me. I'll have to, he won't let me go anywhere without him, he feels kind of maternal towards me. I think he wants to look after someone.

Ha! As if I needed looking after.

There are just about no buses running any more, and those that do are generally on strike or in the workshop or you have to have a machine gun to get aboard, so we decided to walk over to north London. The exercise will do us good, it's only eleven miles. David's idea this is; he made me dump the motorbike, said his guts couldn't stand the strain. We'd have been there in no time on that. No time or never. How many lawmen can you walk past in eleven miles? I try not to think about it, you can't spend all your life a raving paranoid. Mind you, I often wonder what the hell people who aren't paranoid find to think about all day.

I give a sideways glance at David. I daren't describe him to you. Yes I will. He's got a lilac fedora on. I said, 'For chrissake David, I'm trying to look inconspicuous!' I might as well shout at the bloody wind.

He says, 'Don't fret honey, any looks'll be coming my way.' I suppose he's right.

And under that, he's got a kind of red dungaree thing, with a blue, what's that stuff? sheepsucker?

seersucker, that's it – a blue seersucker shirt. And his
dungees are tucked into bright orange boots. And
there's a big lump in the front of his trousers. Which is
his knuckleduster. God, I can't bear to look. Honestly,
it makes your bloody eyes water. It's like walking
down the street with a close encounter.

We set off early and London hasn't altered a bit in
my absence. It's still a city in pursuit of entropy.

Hell, if there was any more litter in the streets people
would be better off living in the bloody dumps. The
roads are coming apart at the seams, the tarmac looks
like it's going through acne. You have to walk through
puddles where mains have burst or the sewers have
puked. They're years behind with the goddamn work,
getting further back all the time. They'll never catch
up. They need to build the city anew. The houses are
just falling down, patched together with anything
people can get hold of. Usually the neighbour's bricks.

It's dismal and depressing. It always looks as though
it has just been raining, do you know what I mean?
People gather on every corner for something to do.
Little gangs of them. It's horrifying. So much distrust
and unease everywhere. You daren't look at anyone in
case they nut you.

They say that if you stand at any intersection in any
of the big cities, within twenty minutes you'll see a
fight. And in half an hour you'll be in one.

God, I wish we were over in America. Hardly the
land of the free any more, but at least it's better than this.

All the shops boarded up. Broken glass grizzling
underfoot. Wounded dogs prowling the streets. Rats.
The inescapable honk of broken sewers. The curfew.
The Pox and the dingoes scowling at every move.
Graffiti on everything that doesn't move, and most of

the things that do. Not even intelligent graffiti, just obscenity. Scatology rules, okay?

It's a land fit for weirdoes.

That goddamn war has got a lot to answer for. Mind you, it might be a damn sight worse if there wasn't a war on. If all the suckers were over here, roaming the streets with nothing to do, what the hell would it be like then?

There are faded war posters falling down everywhere. All the glory has gone now. All the fighting talk, the bravado, the gung-ho! It's down to reality. The mud, the maggots, the bodies without names or faces. God only knows what it must be like in Europe, they've stopped showing us.

The war's just a goddamn farce anyway. It's replaced the flaming Olympics. Except nobody wants to win. They just keep slugging away like two exhausted boxers in the middle of the ring.

The Soviets don't want to win because it would bring them practically into direct contact with the Yanks. They'd be staring at each other across the grey, turgid water, shitting bricks. I mean they could win, any bloody day they liked. But they don't.

And the Yanks won't join in because they're too frightened that they're not as tough as they like to think. So they just stir it up and provoke it endlessly, like some frostbitten old spinster or hungry necrophile. That's their new policy after Central America. Brandishing their fistfuls of rockets, shouting abuse across the waves. 'We'd rather be dead than red!' Oh bleeding kill yourselves then, I don't care.

And what's Britain? It's just a tatty old hedge in between them. Something for the other guys to hide behind. Nobody wants us. I don't know why they don't admit that and pull us out the flaming war. I don't know how folk can keep swallowing the crap time after time. I tell you, there's nothing worse for a country than having a history.

I'll tell you how I see it – I don't think they could stop the goddamn war if they wanted to. Once you've tipped a bucket of blood into a pond, how can you stop it spreading? You can't can you?

God, seventy per cent unemployment. What would it be if there wasn't a war!

Well, I try not to think about all this as I stomp along with my hands pushed through the holes in my pockets. David's gathering lots of whistles. I just grow hot under the collar and wish he'd take his bloody hat off. I think it's the flower that really gets me.

A couple of drunks try to mug us, but before I can yell for help David kicks one in the joint and we barely have to swerve. I keep forgetting I've got Superman with me. We go into a caff for a cup of char, but there are so many goddamn flies and people coughing all over the place we go out again.

How come the whole world isn't dripping with misanthropy? Are people really not that bothered about what other folk get up to in the way of making life a fucking misery? I ask David what he thinks about it all. Someone with a huge lilac fedora ought to have some views.

'I think,' he says, 'it would be a great deal better if the whole scene was disinfected, given a new coat of paint, and ceremonially burned to the ground.'

I grunt. 'How do you stand it?'

He shrugs. 'What can you do?'

He's right. You can't be philosophical in a pisshole. I unwrap another Mars and suck on it gloomily.

I'm just waiting for someone to tell me that Mars Bars give you cancer of the teeth.

We reached the crematorium gardens in Walthamstow where my mother's ashes lie. At least they did, until someone ploughed them all up by mistake. I assume they're still round here somewhere. David took off his hat but waited outside.

I went in feeling like a prick. I'm not a great one for honouring the dead, mysticism, commemoration, all that kind of thing. To tell you the truth, I didn't even know where her flaming brass plate was; I was wandering round for half an hour before I realized they went in years. God, my feet were killing me. I was thinking about stealing a bike to get us home. David made me take a bunch of daffodils, but I got pissed off carrying them and they were starting to droop in the middle, so I stuck them in the first empty pot I came across. Harold Melville. Good luck Harold, wherever you are.

Hundreds of people died the year my mother went. There must have been something going around. The plates were getting smaller and smaller. Pretty soon they'll be etching epitaphs on microscope slides.

I found it eventually and read it unhappily. She had a lousy life. And this was a really weird sort of end. Stuck in here with all these dead brass plates turning green. Dogs cocking their legs. Kids prising them loose to use as skimmers on the pond. It made me feel kind of guilty for being alive. I felt I should be crying and wailing and walking about with my chin on my chest.

I don't know why, I walk like that all the time.

I looked around for David. But he was mooching off

to look at a burial. There's never anyone to share your guilt with.

LOUISE ANNALEE HOWARD 8 JANUARY 1972-12 JUNE 2011

They even had her goddamn name wrong. It was Louisa.

Oh Christ, why do people have to die and leave others behind to remember and feel guilty? Life's bad enough. But that's a mere fleeting thought, there are less anagogic things to consider. For scratched into a corner of the plate like a hurried afterthought, or a visitation from the eerie, is a phone number. I feel sweat prickle on my shoulder blades. I hate mysteries.

I look around nervously, but the few bazonkas present are trying hard to grieve or just looking bored. I squint and try to memorize it, mutter it aloud about a dozen times. Then, forsaking the ghosts, I scurry out to tell David, terrified and intrigued. Something weird is going on here.

Just nipping through the rusty gate I toss a glance back. A figure is standing just about where I stood, perusing the names. A bloody dwarf. Another dwarf. Curiouser and curiouser. If I wasn't so caught up I might have been more interested. But my mind was buzzing too much. Probably nothing to do with me anyway. Life's full of weird coincidences. Let's face it, life *is* a weird coincidence.

I pick up David and we start to walk back. 'Did you see that dwarf?' I ask. He shakes his head. 'Funny that. That guy a few weeks back, the name in the paper – now another one.'

'Perhaps there is always a dwarf in a garden of repose,' he says enigmatically. I think his hat must be too tight.

We're walking slowly past some shops. This isn't far from where I used to live. Place full of unhappy memories. It wasn't far from here that Homer hunted me. We're not talking much, walking and thinking. My mind is miles away. But my eyes are looking for a phone that isn't in kit form. This could take all day.

Suddenly a hand lands on my shoulder. My guts go through a minor seizure. By the cat's bollocks! My heart goes zooming away to a distant part of the universe. I feel my knees dissolve.

'Oh God, Aunty Mel!' I wheeze. 'God you frightened the shit out of me!'

Aunty Mel giggles like a schoolgirl. 'Tee hee hee! I knew it was you, Barty! I thought it was you!' She gives me a big smackeroony on the cheek, bounces me off a bosom that could stop a train. 'I knew it was you!'

I struggle to pull myself together while Mel perfumes the street and smoothes a few lumps out of her stomach with a truly superhuman effort. David looks her up and down quizzically.

'This is David, Aunty Mel,' I mumble. 'A friend of mine.'

Mel offers her hand. But her smile is uncertain. She mutters an aside as though she thinks he's deaf. 'He looks a bit −'

'Yes, he is.'

'Oh Barty! You've not gone −'

'No − he's just a friend. Why don't you walk on ahead David and I'll catch you up?' He nods and moves on. With a certain relief I imagine. Her tangerine hot pants clashed with his red dungees something awful.

'Well, how's tricks Mel?' I see you've got two black eyes.

'Oh, you know!' She laughs. Then bursts into tears,

right in the middle of the goddamn street. 'Bloody awful Barty! They're bloody awful!'

Hell's teeth! I steer her towards a bar. 'Let's go and get a drink Mel. Don't let everyone see you like that.'

'I'm sorry Barty! I'm sorry!' She blubbers into the tiniest handkerchief you ever saw. It looks like a fairy's nappy. You couldn't squeeze a blackhead with it. 'I'm sorry Barty, I'm sorry!'

'Mind the step Mel. Sit down there. Mind where you put your bag. What do you want – gin? brandy?'

'Just a pint Barty, just a pint.'

'A pint? A pint of what? Gin?' A moment of panic.

She giggles, the tears in her eyes light up. 'Don't be silly Barty. Mackeson.'

I fetch the drinks while Mel looks around for a mirror, wobbles over to tidy herself up. I watch her pull her stomach in, her bottom; she stretches her neck until there are only two chins. Oh God, poor old Mel. I sit down and she gives me a cigarette bloody with lipstick. She pats my knee.

'Sorry about that Barty. I couldn't help it. I was just so pleased to see you. I thought you were in gaol and –'

I nearly choke on my beer. 'Ssh! Don't tell everyone!'

'Oh!' Aunt Mel looks surprised. 'Oh, I see. You mean, you're –?' I nod. 'Oh, I see.' She thinks this over, I can hear her brain struggling out of the blankets. She downs her pint at a second attempt. 'That beer's warm.'

'What happened to your face, Aunt Mel?'

'This?' Her fingertips try to hide the stains. 'Nothing.' She pauses like a cliché, letting moments slide away as if they're not suitable. Then she finds one to her liking, blurts. 'Oh God Barty, you've got to help me! It's Gerald, he's killing me!'

'Gerald? I thought you'd eat his sort for breakfast.' She could crush him between her bazonkas.

'No Barty. No. I'm serious. I mean it. He's a sadist. He makes me buy things, belts and straps and things, so he can hit me with them. I'm black and blue all over Barty. I've got broken bones and all sorts. Look. . . .'

I make her put it away. This was crazy. Was she being serious? 'Why don't you just sling him out?'

'I can't Barty, I can't! He goes – berserk! He's like a mad dog!'

I started sipping beer to give me time to think. What the hell is this? I've only just met her after, what? nearly two years. I can't even think this quickly, I couldn't make sense of what she was saying.

'Don't run out on me Barty. You're the only person I know.'

I rubbed my face and went to get another couple of drinks. While I was gone she got a handbag mirror out and changed the shape of her face. She looked younger when I returned. She smiled, a cloud of her toothpaste breath steamed over me. It must be something she keeps in her handbag. But it was a strained smile, like she was really desperate for my help.

'It's all a bit much is it?'

I smile helplessly.

'I'm not getting any younger Barty, am I?'

'You're doing fine, Mel. You look pretty good.'

'Pretty good! I look like an old queen! It's the only way I know how.' She lit a cigarette and, God, her whole body was trembling. This was really unsettling. I didn't know how I was supposed to react. I'm a bit impotent when it comes to social intercourse.

43

'You've changed, Barty. You're not so shy any more. You're older. Harder.'

'Am I?' Am I? I hadn't thought about it. Maybe she's right. Older. Sadder. Wiser. I don't feel any wiser. But I suppose it must change you, being on the Canal. It would modify a saint.

She nods. 'Yeah. You used to be a kid. You don't blush at me any more!'

She's pretty wise Aunt Mel, you have to give her credit for that. I tried to change the subject. 'I've just been to see Ma's plate.'

'Oh yeah,' as if she knew. She wasn't concentrating.

'You want to watch it, Barty. People round here, they'll turn you in for the price of a fag-end.'

'Yes, I know.'

'You can't trust anyone. Look at Gerald. Who'd have thought a weedy little guy like that. . . . He's been put away for it before you know.'

'Beating people up?'

'Bigamy.'

'Bigamy! You're not married to him are you?'

She nods. 'Me and two others.'

'Jesus Christ, Mel! Why don't you just tell the police? They'll get rid of him for you.'

'I can't Barty,' pleading. 'He'd kill me. He's a nasty person, he's got a wicked streak in him.'

'Well I don't see what I can do. I mean, he looks pretty hard to me. I don't want to get smashed up.'

'Haven't you got a gun?'

'I'm not Billy the Kid you know.'

'Please Barty, you've got to do something. I'll let you – you know.'

'It's not that, Mel.' In fact I'd rather do without it to be honest. 'It's just – he'd murder me.'

'No he wouldn't Bart. You can look after yourself.'

'I can't Mel. People are always beating me up. Look at my face!'

'Your face is lovely, Barty.'

Oh God, don't say that Mel, you know what I'm like. I start to writhe, indecision tosses me like a coin. Heads I lose, tails I lose.

'I've never asked you for anything, Barty.'

'I know that Mel.'

'I just want you to be there. The two of us together, we can do it.'

'I think you'd be better off with the law.'

'Not with his sort, Barty. Let's have another drink. Have a whisky, give yourself some Butch courage.'

'Dutch courage.' They don't stock that much whisky Mel. I sigh, buy another pair of drinks. Half an hour later we're ready to make love, fall asleep or sing the Irish rebel songs. But I'm still not ready to tackle Gerald. It needs more than whisky to open the door on my cowardice.

'Barty – if you help me, I'll tell you something about someone you know.'

'Me?' I slur. 'Who the hell do I know?'

'Someone from – when you were in trouble before.'

Oh God, she's playing games. 'I don't know anybody. Who?'

'An albino.'

My blood turns to gas. A screaming starts up deep in my belly, floods up my spine to my brain. 'Homer?' I gasp. But only my ears hear it.

'Homer?'

She nods, happily.

'Holy Christ. What about him Mel, what about the guy?'

'If you help me, I'll tell you.'

Christ, you bitch! I glare at her as if she's just given me gonorrhoea, totting up odds in my head.

'Hang on a minute!' I lumber out. Return a minute later, knock a couple of glasses over, trembling like I've got the DTs. But I feel suddenly quite sober. Horribly so. David's knuckleduster is lumpy in my pocket. Some quick advice on when to duck is yammering in my brain.

'Oh God, I hope you know what we're doing, Mel.' Please don't let him hurt me.

Perhaps he'll have a heart attack before we get there. He will if prayers count for anything.

We climb the stairs to Mel's apartment quietly. I'm so quiet, I wonder if I'm still downstairs. But the pad is empty.

I take my first breath for ten minutes. My heart remembers how to beat. 'You've had it redecorated then?' I say as she closes the door. 'What colour's this?'

'It's avocado green and midnight purple.'

'Is it? You could do with a few searchlights around the place.' You couldn't see a bloody thing.

She slid her coat off, looked in a mirror. There were so many mirrors around it was like being a dragonfly. 'Sit down, Barty. He won't be long. I'll make us a cup of tea shall I?'

I nodded. Put a barricade up while you're out there; a big one.

'What do you want me to do, Mel? Should I just tell him to clear off, or what?'

'Well I'll get his things together in a minute. That

won't take long!' she said scornfully. 'Then we'll leave it by the door and – just, tell him.

'What do you think about this T-shirt, Barty? Not too obvious is it?'

'No. It covers your nipples.' When you breathe out.

She shook her head. 'I don't know. I think I'll have to do something about this chest. It's getting to be a liability. Kids keep grabbing hold of it.' I'm not surprised, you keep sticking it in their faces. I rolled a cigarette, saw my hands blur they were trembling so much.

Mel disappeared to cram Gerald's gear into a plastic bag and I tried to think of something cheerful. Piles are cheerful compared with the way I was feeling.

I shot from the seat like a hot flea when the front door opened and Gerald belched in, stinking as though he'd just had a bath in ale. He eyed me shiftily, snarled something indecipherable, looked around the room for something.

'You see me fags?'

I shook my head.

He sniffed. 'Gis one then.'

I stood my ground. I had a kind of paralysis. Come on Mel, where the piss are you? He wasn't as big as I remembered, he just looked – nasty. I glanced at his hands. Just as I feared – callouses.

'What you doing here anyway? I thought you'd pissed off.'

'I've come to sling you out.' The words fell out before I could check them. Tact you need, you stupid bastard, tact. Talk your way out of it. God, I'll cut this bloody tongue out.

'You have have you?'

'Aye. So why don't you just get your things and go.' What I'd give for a voice that doesn't quaver.

47

'Why don't you sod off?'

'I don't want any trouble –'

'Well frig off then.'

I slipped my hand into the dusters in my pocket, stuck my hand behind my back. I had a feeling something was about to happen. Come on Mel, for chrissake.

He looked around again, uninterestedly, then he made a lunge at me. I jumped away like a goosed wallaby – I was expecting it but it was still a surprise – and he swung a suicidally wild punch at my nose. I mean, it's a big nose, but it's not that big. He wouldn't have hit an elephant.

I sidestepped, slammed my fist into the point of his ribs, just where David said. He dropped with a thunderous gasp and I spun away with tears in my eyes. God, I felt like I'd broken every bone in my wrist. I strutted about the room shaking my hand and biting my lip off, while Gerald rolled about whooping for breath, hooting. We looked like a couple of Caribbean disco dancers. His face was as twisted as a pretzel.

Aunt Mel suddenly appeared, tiptoed into the room like a bipedal blancmange, hoofed Gerald in the crutch. Even I felt sorry for the guy then. He screamed. He was having a private battle with himself, snorting, punching the floor, clawing at himself. Aunt Mel had no sympathy. She kicked him again, ran to the door, lobbed his stuff down the stairs.

She came back into the room, grabbed Gerald by the hair, began dragging him towards the door. 'Get his feet, Barty!'

Get his feet? Is she blind? My wrist is fractured in a dozen places!

I copped hold of an ankle with my good hand, we wrestled him to the landing.

48

We threw him down the stairs.

Back in the flat I collapsed into a chair and felt sick. All the blood seemed to drain out of my body. 'Well done Barty, well done!' said Mel, and she checked her hair in a mirror. 'Well done!' I stuck my head between my knees.

I didn't stay around too long after that. I had that phone call to make. I didn't have much to say to Mel. The only thing I could talk about was working on the Canal. And all she knew was how difficult it is to get a bra to fit these days.

So after about half an hour and a couple of coffees I stood up to leave.

'Will you come back, Barty? Don't go off again for years, not now you've come back.'

No, I promised I wouldn't. I said I'd look her up every time I was in the area.

I stepped out of the front door. And Gerald hammered me with a bottle. I went down like the *Titanic*. Nothing could save me. I bounced down eighteen stairs. Fortunately I wasn't awake to realize that, the blow knocked all the senses out of the front of my brain. I can just remember seeing the stairs looming up to greet me.

I must have been counting black sheep for some time. When I came round I was akimbo on Mel's bed, and these two amazing chandeliers were hanging over me. Only they weren't chandeliers, they were Mel's breasts, sprinkled with glitter-dust.

I don't know which was worse, the road accident in the side of my head, or the thought that those two enormous bazonkas were going to bounce the life out of me.

Mel smoothed my hair. 'Does it hurt, Barty? Is it very bad?'

I tried to nod. But my face was too stiff. 'Has he gone?' A frog croaked on my behalf.

She nodded. 'Yes. He won't be coming back now. We'd just hurt his pride, that was all. He'll be all right now.'

I give another of my imperceptible inclinations. 'You've got no clothes on Mel.'

She tittered. 'I wondered if you'd notice!' With all that glitter-dust, satellite telescopes were probably homing in. I winced as she swung astride me, like a dirigible caught in a crosswind. Oh no, not now Mel, I've got a splitting headache. But once she's made her mind up. . . .

A curtain descends. Even Beekay likes some privacy you know.

I'd have had to come back anyway. In all the excitement I'd forgotten what I really came for.

'Mel? What about Homer?'

'Who?'

'The albino.'

'Oh yes.' She yawned, capsized out of bed, padded across the wolfskin rug to the pink dressing table. She looks twice as big when she's got no clothes on. 'He left something for you.'

'For me? Did he say anything? When did you see him? Did he come here?'

'Yes, he came here a few weeks ago. Said he was a friend of yours from the old days.'

'What did he look like? Was he in one piece?'

She was rooting through a drawer. Curlers, roll-ons, all sorts of nightmares tumbled out. 'He looked – *weird*! He's got no hair, he's got a big scar across his cheek, he limps, and there's something wrong with one of his arms. He looks like he's been in a haccident.'

A haccident? It's a pity it wasn't fatal. 'What did he want?'

'He said, "Have you seen Beekay?" I said, "Beekay who?" as if I didn't know. "What's it got to do with you?" "I'm a friend of his," says he. "A friend from the old days. You tell him, if you see him, that his old mate Homer is around. And he'll look him up." And then he said, if I see you, to give you this. I don't know what it is,' she held it up. 'Looks like a piece of something.'

It was a bullet. And it looked plastic. The end of it was red. But I knew what it was. Harry told me about them. It was a radiation bullet; arabs they're called. They've started using them in the war. A weapon of fear.

'Don't play with it, Mel! Get rid of it! Flush it down the toilet!'

'It's only a little toy!'

'It's not a toy, Mel! It's dangerous! Bloody danger-ous!' She shrugged, tossed it into an ashtray. 'Not there for chrissake! Down the toilet!'

'All right, don't shout!' She waddled out in a huff. A Christmas turkey looking for its feathers.

I was trembling all over. So what's new in that you ask? This time I've got reason.

That's what Homer is going to do. He's going to kill me – with cancer.

FIVE

I cleared my throat, squinted as the number purred like a mechanical cat. It sounded as though no one was ever going to answer. Twelve times it rang into eternity.

Someone picked up the phone. Nobody said anything, very quietly. 'Hello – is Gay there?' There was no response. Just a listening. I heard the silent someone lay down the receiver with a clunk, then there came the creaking of feet counting stairs.

'Hello? Hello?'

I heard a bombination, murmuring, then the phone was picked up again. But still nobody spoke. Maybe I've dialled a heavy-breather. Perhaps it's a home for the mute.

'Gay?' This kind of thing really fazes me.

I listened to a tiny rustling noise, a sound like a tissue getting ready to sneeze, then a pixie whispered out of the earpiece. 'Is that Beekay?'

'Yeah, who is that? Where's Gay?'

'She's here. But she's not well.'

'What do you mean she's not well? Who is that?'

'Are you in a call-box?'

'Yes.'

'Come to twenty-seven, Athelstone Road.' Then she hung up. A wordthrift.

'Hello?' I don't know why I bothered doing that, but they always do it on the telly.

I turned to David, listening over my shoulder. 'What the hell's going on?'

He shrugged. 'Life's full of mysteries.' Just what I need, a walking cliché.

Athelstone Road is your average drag. It's stuffed with ho-hum shops and houses, no front gardens, lots of grids and the shadows of dog piss on the walls, like doors to secret worlds.

We watch it for a long time, David, Ron, me. We don't trust anybody. Any little kid looks at us for too long we're ready to shoot him. 'What do you think?' I ask at last.

David squints. 'Can't tell, can you? Could be full of furies.'

'That kid keeps going in and out.'

'They could be working him by strings.'

'What should we do then?'

'You're the boss, Beak. We'll do what you suggest.' He thought about it. 'As long as it's not stupid.'

I haven't got any bloody suggestions have I? I don't know what to do. I squeeze the gun in my pocket and pummel my brain. Come on goddammit, wake up!

'Maybe we could send a message in,' said Ron.

David became sarcastic. 'What do we say, "any police in there, please signal"?'

'All right, I'll go in then. No one knows me do they?'

David and I look at each other, after some contemplation agree. 'But keep your gun handy,' I said. 'And if there's any trouble just beat it.' Full of advice I am.

'I won't be giving encores.'

'Here's that kid again,' said David.

I accost him. 'Hey kid, do you know a girl called Gay, lives over there?'

'Yeah. Top floor.' Then he ran off, with a piece of chewing gum stuck to his foot.

Ron buckled his belt a macho hole tighter. Checked his pistol. Sauntered over the road.

We all have poppers now. They were easy enough to obtain. I just went out after curfew one night and pretended to be drunk. Two young sharpies turn up, start pushing me around a bit; it's easier to rough people up than arrest them, you don't need to be able to write then. While I'm staggering about groaning, David and Ron creep up behind, lay them out with table legs, hand in the holster and we're away.

We peep out cautiously until Ron reappears. He's very nonchalant. I envy him his lack of hysteria. My stomach is full of slamming doors.

'Just two janeys in a room at the back. One of them's sick.'

I cross the road like fast. Crash up the stairs.

'Gay?'

There's a girl standing by a yellow wall, looking scared to death. A waif of a girl in an orange dress. Hair hanging straight down to her shoulders in a cheap style, badly cut. Eyes from a rabbit. Mouth open in alarm.

'Gay?' She's on a cot, lying on her side. She smiles.

'Hello Beak.'

I grab hold of her as hard as I dare, she doesn't look well. She's as frail as frosty grass. 'Gay?' She bursts into tears and I start crying. David and Ron shuffle uncomfortably, the girl relaxes, gets a chair from somewhere, gives it to Ron. David sits on a chest of drawers and looks worried to hell. We just carry on crying for a long time.

'How have you been, Beak?' she asks at last.

'Me?' I snuffle. 'Okay, you know. How about you – you don't look so good.' I tried to smile.

She tried to laugh, looked across to the girl, who turned away, started counting clouds out of the window. Then she looked at me again. Turned those bruised unhappy eyes like harbingers of some terrible fate and said, 'I've got leukaemia, Beak. I'm dying.'

What do you say at a moment like that? I didn't say anything. I almost vomited to be honest. Everything inside my stomach slipped a notch.

A terrible silence poked its head around the door and coughed into the room. 'Leukaemia?' I whispered at last, and my voice tripped over the step at the back of my throat. 'Leukaemia?'

Gay nodded, turned away, released a great sigh. 'I've had it for five months now.'

'But can't they cure it? Can't they do something?' She shook her head.

'They must give you something for it. They must be able to do something.' Why am I so angry?

She didn't take any notice of me. She'd probably been through it all herself. 'Acute granulocytic leukaemia,' she said. 'There's no cure.'

I didn't know what to do. I sat on the bed and held her hand, squeezed her arm. I tried to think of something brilliant.

'Who are your friends, Beak?'

'David and Ron. David was an overseer on the Canal, but he wasn't suited to the work. He helped me get away.'

'Hello,' said David. Ron smiled.

'You're quite a hero, Beak.'

'Me?'

'Amongst the criminal element! You get great write-ups in the underground press!'

'Do I?' I let out a small laugh. But the air didn't suit it and it expired quickly.

'Don't look so worried Beak, I'm not going to die right now!'

'But – I don't want you to die at all!' I started to cry again. David began crying.

Then Gay started again. 'I wouldn't have brought you here if I'd known you were going to be like this!' she laughed, cried. The room watched sadly.

'Do you want a drink, Gay?' whispered the girl.

Gay nodded. 'I have to drink a lot,' she said to me. 'My throat gets very dry and sore. This is Jasmine by the way, a good friend of mine.'

Jasmine smiled nervously and nodded. 'I'll go and make some tea for us all,' she whispered.

'I'll give you a hand,' said David and he followed her out, leading Ron. They were holding hands tightly.

They closed the door and I sat there holding the hand of my girl, who seemed only half the size she used to be. She was nearly thirty, but she looked like a sick child, bruised and wan and tired.

I ransacked my brain looking for something to say. I was so – disappointed. So sad. That it should all end like this. . . .

I just kept shaking my head. She was so tiny. She looked as though starvation was her lover. The copper hair had shed all its lustre; still cropped short, but thinner now, pale where the scalp pressed wearily through. There was a sheen on her forehead as if a fever had emerged momentarily for a breath of fresh air.

I looked down at her hand, so ridiculously small. You couldn't hold anything in that. Poor Gay, her nails looked so pale and brittle. . . .

'What are you thinking?'

'I was just looking at your hands.'

She held one up to look at it. 'They're pathetic aren't they? I should donate them to a squirrel or something. A hamster.'

'How have you been keeping – really?'

She sighed. 'There's not much you can do. I go to the hospital once a week, get an injection. And I take pills.' She showed me a drawerful of pill-pots.

'Where do you get the money from for all of these?'

'Jasmine gets it for me,' she said quietly.

'Where did you meet her?'

'We hid in the same place when we were running from the prison! That was quite a stunt! I didn't know you went in for things like that.'

'You know me. Anything for a laugh.'

'There is no cure Beak,' she said seriously. 'They can belt you with radiation, give you some remission. A few weeks maybe, a couple of months –'

'Isn't that worth it? Don't you want to stay alive?'

'Beak, what's the point of being alive if you're life is – a bloody hell? Just being conscious – it isn't reward enough. Not when you hurt all the time. Not when your body's falling to bits in front of your eyes,' she whispered. 'It gets worse all the time.

'I don't want to lose you, Beak. I don't want to die. Christ, we've had little enough time together as it is. But there must be some pleasure in life, mustn't there? It must have some – quality.

'Don't look so sad. You don't want me to be unhappy, do you?'

'I don't know! I can't believe there's nothing can be done. There must be something –'

'There's nothing, Beak. Christ, I've read every book I can find on it. There's nothing. I'll probably last another couple of months. I'll get the flu or something, that'll be it.' She shrugged. 'It won't be too bad.'

I tried to smother a choke. A couple of months? Jesus Christ, Gay – what are they doing to you? I felt tears trickling out of my eyes again, tried to shake them away, blinking like a madman.

'Will you stop crying for chrissake! Go and tell the others to bring the tea, they're downstairs at the end of the hall.

'Then you can tell us how you got away from that prison escort. It's like the Wild West, reading about you in the papers!'

It's a really awful thing, watching someone die.

Gay slept on the bed, I was on the floor beside her, Jasmine slept curled up in the armchair, and David and Ron slept on cushions on the landing.

And, like people in the foyer of a theatre of death, we hung around and – waited for Gay to die.

Eventually David and Ron rented a room not far away, but they still came around every evening. We used to play cards, the five of us. Playing cards until the sleep dripped out of our eyes.

I used to get really upset about it all. I'd get angry, and start shouting at Jasmine, down in the kitchen. But she just let me. I couldn't understand this disease. I couldn't see it or grapple with it. She didn't look that sick. She seemed to be dying under false pretences.

58

'I just can't understand it. I don't know – anything about it.'

'There's not much to know. You get it, you get sick, you die.'

'But why her? It doesn't seem fair.'

'It never seems fair.'

'Oh, Jesus Christ.' I'm being taught philosophy by a bloody kid.

'She loved you while she could. You loved her. That has to be enough.'

'It can't be enough. The world's bad enough without dying like this!'

'You can't do anything, Beekay. It's the way of it.'

'I know I can't do anything! That doesn't make me feel any fucking better!'

Gay lasted seven more weeks.

She didn't get the flu or anything like that. She haemorrhaged internally.

Oh God – I can't tell you about that. The panic, the screams – just forget it. She died. It's not something you'd want to hear.

Jasmine and I pulled the pictures down, moved out of the room and took an attic cubicle a few blocks from our homo buddies.

Poor Gay, we couldn't even have her cremated under her right name. Margaret Talbot, that's who they burned. Margaret Talbot. Burned in a hardboard coffin.

You'll notice that I have another one to take care of now. Gay wanted me to look after Jasmine. 'She's got nowhere to go, Beak. She doesn't have anyone. All her family are dead.'

'She must have friends somewhere.'

'We're all her friends, Beak. She needs you.'

'But I can't have her trailing along, Gay. She's only a kid. How old is she, fifteen, sixteen? It's hard enough as it is. I don't even know anything about her. What was she put away for?'

'She murdered her uncle.'

'Oh great!'

'He used to rape her, Beak. He did –' she pulled a face – 'all sorts of things.'

I tried not to weaken. 'So what did she do, club him to death with her hockey stick?'

'She cut his throat.'

'Cut his throat! Oh come on Gay, you must be –'

'She's really a gentle girl, Beak.'

'Gentle! Well thank Christ she's not the violent sort,

we'd all be having a Caesarean on our bloody windpipes!'

'Look, she likes you.'

I turned around. Jasmine was about fifteen feet away, giving me this really nervous smile, all trepid and hopeful and trusting and – oh Christ, what chance have you got?

So she tags along behind me now. We don't sleep together or anything like that. Actually, I don't get a lot of sex at all. I get hardly any. Maybe less than that. She has the bed and I sleep on a mattress on the floor. She's only about four feet ten, she could practically sleep on the pillow. When she snores it's like the door of a doll's house creaking in the wind.

I suppose it's kind of cute really.

SEVEN

The year reached June and it was muggy; lots of flies, lots of thunder. We were coming back from the pub one lunchtime, me and Jasmine, having an argument. We've been having a lot or arguments lately. Usually along the lines of why aren't I doing something constructive about getting us all out of this pisshole and off to America?

'Oh don't go on about it all the time. I'm doing my best.'

'Wha' are you doin'? You're not doin' bloody anythink, are you?'

'I am, I am! I'm thinking about it.'

'Well that's all you're doin', 'cos you ain't *doin'* nothink, are you?'

'It's not that bloody easy you know! I suppose you think it's fucking simple! What do you want me to do, walk into a bloody nick and say "Look, me and a couple of mates tried to blow up a prison a couple of years ago and we got caught, but I got away, and I want to find out where my mates are so I can rescue them!" I suppose you think that's how to do it, hey, hey?'

'I don't know how you're gonna do it, you're the one with the flamin' brains! But you ain't doin' nothink are you? You're just mopin' around, moanin' all the time! We're never gonna get anywhere at this rate! We'll be here for bloody years!'

'Oh that's fucking good! Fucking good that is, isn't

it? I didn't have to take you on you know! I could have just bloody dumped you!'

Jasmine snorted. 'Oh big deal! You big girl's blouse!'

'Look Jasmine, if I knew what was the best thing to do, I'd bloody do it, wouldn't I? But I don't yet! So there's no point just barging in until we know just what it is we should be bloody doing.'

'An' is that gonna be before we draw our pensions or after?' She's a little bitch sometimes.

'Look, I've got a couple of ideas that I'm –'

'No you 'aven't! You 'aven't got no ideas! You're just scared, that's all!' She put a lot of scorn into that one. 'You've turned bloody chicken, 'aven't you? You're too scared to do anythink in case you get caught, ain't you? So you're just gonna prat about, an' these two big mates of yours that you're always on about, you're just gonna forget 'em, ain't you? If they've got them workin' on the Canal, they'll have bloody turned up by the time you do anythink! But it's all right for you, innit, you're out now! You don't care do you?'

'Of course I bloody care!'

'No you don't! You don't care about any of us! It's just a big con, we're never gonna get to America, are we? Never ever.'

'Soddin' hell Jasmine, if you think it's so fucking easy, you come up with something! Just stop moaning all the time and bloody do something!'

'Well I will! I'll go down the bloody office an' tell 'em I'm his sister an' I wanna go visit 'im!'

'He hasn't got any sisters.'

'You're just lookin' for excuses ain't you? You're turnin' chicken! We're never gonna get to America! You just lied to us!'

63

'Oh – shut your gob!' I stormed in through the front door and pounded up the stairs.

'Don't you tell me to shut me gob!' She came pounding up the stairs behind me.

We got to the second landing, a few feet away from our room. And suddenly it blew up.

A piece of the door caught me in the cheek and I span away with a cry. Jasmine screamed. There was a great whumph! Dust and flame ripped the door off its hinges and pinned it against the opposite wall. The house shook.

I staggered back into Jasmine and she caught me. What the hell was it, gas? It couldn't be gas, we haven't got any. It must be a bomb! I flung Jasmine down the stairs, fell after her. 'What is it?' she screamed. 'What are you doing?'

'A bomb,' I muttered.

We raced down the final flight and out into the street. Quite a crowd had gathered – always pulls a big crowd, an explosion. Standing there with their mouths hanging open, catching snowflakes. But the only things they'd be catching would be bits of my shirts, fluttering down on the breeze.

I looked up. The front of the house had been blown out; a hole had been blasted in the roof. The landlady was going to go crackers.

'What about our stuff?'

'Forget it.'

I stopped suddenly. Somebody wasn't looking up with the rest. He was looking at me. Straight at me. Looking at me, and grinning.

It was a dwarf. Standing just across the street, his hands in the pockets of a tiny blue jacket. He had his hair greased back, and he was laughing. His mouth was twisted open, and he was laughing mirthlessly, without any sound, rocking on his heels.

Jasmine saw him too. 'Who's he?' she whispered.

I shook my head. 'I don't know.'

He turned away and sauntered off down the street with his dwarf's walk, with his baggy white trousers tumbling in a succession of folds to his boots, laughing all the way, until he disappeared.

I wanted to follow him. But I couldn't. He put the fear of God into me.

EIGHT

Somebody shot Aunt Mel.

They shot her at the flat. Put bullet holes in her stomach and her shoulder. I didn't find out about it for a few days, then I went with Jaz up to the hospital at Whipps Cross, where they took her.

She was in one of the cheapest wards you can get. God, it was a fucking nightmare.

I said to her, for chrissake Mel, why the fuck didn't she get something better, Uncle Franklyn must have left her plenty of dough? (Sorry about this anacoluthon, I get a bit confused sometimes.) Gerald spent it. That little bastard. What a git.

What a bloody loser she is. Bloody Mel couldn't win if she was the only horse in the goddamn race. I could have thumped her. She's so dumb. She makes a chicken look smart.

She looked pathetic lying there in her gaudy drabness. Tearful, happy to see someone. No one had visited her. People don't visit women like Mel. People like Mel are forgotten as soon as the door closes. They're like children. We stood looking at her for ages, I couldn't think of anything to say. I suppose I feel some affection for her. But not a great deal. It's mostly guilt. I'm not a great family man. I'd make a lousy father.

God she was a state. Her hair looked about ready to drop out, the grey roots were pushing all the pinky gold aside, it was greasy and stiff. There was a huge green bruise down the side of her face where she'd fallen on a table on her way to the ground. Her skin was covered with venules.

She was still on a saline drip. She couldn't eat or drink; the flesh had deserted her like she was a sinking ship. Loose folds of skin jostled for space all over her arms. The sheets were dirty. I looked around. I hate things like this, I really do.

The whole place was a dump. It was sordid; there were blood stains on all the sheets. Flies were crawling over the beds. People had been sick on the floor. Heaps of rat poison between the beds. Dead mice. Fluff under the beds. I couldn't stand it.

Mel just kept whimpering and clutching my hand. I didn't know what the hell to say to her.

'Did you see who shot you Mel?'

She shook her head. 'I was in the kitchen. And I heard a noise. So I turned round – the living-room was all dark, there was no light on in there, I must've. . . .' She couldn't remember what she must've. 'There was a bang, and something hit me in the shoulder, and I fell on the floor. And then, they shot me again, in the stomach.'

The bullet had a bastard of a time in her guts. Smashed all her kidney to bits, ripped half the intestine to pieces. She had about eighty-six stitches in her. She wanted to show me, but I wouldn't let her.

'Have the police done anything?'

'They haven't been able to send anyone round yet. They've been too busy.' She looked lorn. 'They haven't even got a mirror in here, Barty.'

'I'll get you one.'

'Do I look awful Barty, do I, do I look awful?'

'You're the best one in here,' I lied. She looked like a

bloody vampire. 'You look like a queen.' She laughed. 'Does it hurt?'

'My arm throbs all the time. It's like rheumatism.'

My feet were starting to ache so I sat on the bottom of the bed, between the stains. 'It might be, because of me, you know. It could be the albino, trying to get at me.'

'But why would he want to hurt me? I haven't done anything.' She started pulling eyelashes out with her fingertips.

'Because he's a psychopath. He plays,' I tried to gel the feelings that Homer instils in me, 'sick games. He's a cat with – sadism.' I could tell by her eyes she didn't know what I meant. 'I think you ought to move. Maybe you could go and stay with someone. What about your sister?'

'Vi? In Southend? I don't want to go there, Barty. All that mud. All that bird-poo.'

'Just for a while. Until it's all cleared up.' She pulled a face, winced. 'He might come back, Mel.'

'I thought, maybe it was Gerald.'

'I can't see Gerald being that crazy. He'd got all your flaming money! Whoever it was, they didn't try to kill you, did they Mel? They – just shot you to hurt you.' It sounded horrific and cruel to say it, but I wanted to frighten her. 'That's pretty sick. Gerald would just have pasted you.'

Mel pushed a few tears over her red lids. Not an avalanche, just a few loose boulders. 'How did you get into all this, Barty? How did you get mixed up in it all? Was it Uncle Frank, was it his fault?'

'No, it wasn't Franklyn's fault.'

'He wasn't a bad sort really, Barty.'

Oh come on Mel, don't start getting maudlin. He

68

was a bloody greaseball. 'Do you need any money?'

'No, they just rob it from you when you're asleep.'

The world is a goddamn dungheap, do you know that? A goddamn dungheap.

I hear cholera has broken out in Junk City.

NINE

I found a cart to transport Mel to the station. We could tote her bags for her, but she was in no condition to walk any distance.

She knew as she left the tenny that she wouldn't be coming back there. Once you're seen leaving a place with a suitcase, that's it. The furniture will be gone before you reach the end of the street. By morning a family of squatters will be entrenched. It's a miracle the place wasn't cleared out while she was at the Whip.

Jaz and I helped Mel down the steps. A street full of silent watchers was watching silently. The loudest noise was a curious mutter, until a fart won hands down. That was from one of the kids who had the cart. There were two of them, one about fifteen, the other nearly twenty.

They didn't offer to assist. They probably didn't even think of it. They just slouched there, sneering. I've noticed that a lot of people without any brain compensate by having a sneer.

David and Ron lugged down the cases and stashed them in the cart. They were going to stay behind to start clearing the flat, while Jaz and I went to the station with Mel. It was a kind of tacit understanding that we'd sell as much of the junk as we could and forward the money to her.

A little girl with a nose full of snot marched up

accusingly as we guided Mel's unsteady feet across the flags. 'What's the matter with her?'

'Fuck off.' I really love kids.

The two rays of sunshine stirred themselves as we reached the cart. Dreadful skin colour. They looked more unhealthy than half of the people in the hospital. They looked like they ate germs for breakfast. Covered in spots.

'You haven't got cholera have you?'

'You what?'

'Never mind. Have you got something for her to sit on?'

The younger one looked round dumbly while his elder partner ignored us altogether. 'Er – yeah. There's a piece o' rag.' He pulled out a cloth from somewhere and climbed into the cart to spread it out. It was about as clean as a coal miner's handkerchief.

Boom, a rifle shot screamed out, echoing off the walls of the street. The kid dived into my arms. Most of him, the top of his head had gone missing. I was drenched with blood and brain as it came slopping over the rim of his skull. I slumped to the ground yelling, with his dead weight twitching and kicking like an angry dancer, powering down on me in some awful embrace. I got a mouthful of his blood.

The street emptied. Jaz and Mel were crouched beside the cart, shrieking. David and Ron too. But they weren't shrieking, they were just screaming. The lad's headstuff kept pumping out on me like mulligatawny soup. My hands were sticky with it. I tried to push his useless body away. Both his eyes were hanging out on ladders of slime.

His buddy just stood there, rigid with shock. A sitting duck for any more hungry bullets. But we just left him – no one was going to get killed on his account. This isn't the movies you know.

He wasn't the only sitting duck. The tiny wooden cart was no protection at all. We couldn't even all fit behind it. It was so rotten a woodworm could stab us to death.

The guy who fired was still at the fourth-storey window of the tenny block opposite. We could see him. Still crouched behind his rifle. He obviously hadn't finished yet. The dead kid beside me seemed to be hissing. I was kneeling in his urine.

I don't know who decided it (except it sure as fuck wasn't me) or whether it just happened, but all of a sudden everyone exploded into action. Mel and Jaz scampered for the tenny, Ron threw himself round one end of the cart, David pushed me round the other, dragged me across the road towards the killing house opposite. Why they wanted to kill themselves, and me, was beyond my startled comprehension, and for a moment I pulled back. Why didn't we just run for it? But perhaps they knew that a bullet in the face is better than a bullet in the back. It was no place to argue, particularly as David had just pushed me ahead. I ran. I started to scream and I ran like a scalded whippet.

Halfway across the street Ron fell. His neck opened up for a second bullet. He squealed, bounced off the tarmac, slid into the gutter like a cringing dog. Blood was spitting out of his teeth, pouring out of his throat. He clawed at the kerb. He seemed to be snorting fine red spray from his nostrils.

But we didn't stop. We couldn't. We dived through the swing doors, got in each other's way and fell over in the hall, scrambled up the first two flights of stairs like we were racing. Then we stopped.

Everything went quiet. We crouched in the shadows, panting.

Eighteen feet above us, a killer with a rifle waited. We were petrified. We were stuck. My bladder screamed.

A minute passed. A second. The bird cries of shouting drifted in from outside, but nobody came in the swinging doors. Nobody in the block itself made a sound. Except me and David with our rasping, frightened breathing and our thudding hearts.

We could hear someone moving about, up the stairwell. The slayer. We could hear him shuffling. He was on the landing too. Listening. Eighteen feet. Concrete steps. Thin metal railings. Death.

Didn't know what to do. We just looked at each other, our nostrils wide with fear. Frightened to stir. A lump digging into my side became increasingly painful. Then I recalled what it was. The grenade in my pocket. The last of our souvenirs from Leighton Buzzard.

I pushed the lift button. For maybe the second time in my life, the lift came. It was the day for my gods to take the floor. My hands started to tremble like those tiny dogs, shewotsits. I couldn't swallow. My stomach was ready to leave.

I pushed the button for the fourth floor, tore out the pin, placed the grenade. We flattened ourselves against the wall. The lift clunked and creaked, whirred its lonely way upwards. It clanked past the third floor, trundled to the fourth. The grenade should be just about ready to destroy itself, all those years of waiting about to end – the doors hissed as a prelude to opening, the elevator clearing its throat –

Boom!! The bottom of the lift went clattering and screaming down the shaft. Mummy, Mummy, someone blew me up! Lumps of cement and metal tumbled down the stairwell. Then there was silence, except that a piece of something couldn't decide whether to fall off and was cricking against something else. Crick. Crick. Crick.

We waited. In a way we were no better off, we still didn't dare go up there.

But after about a minute, balls of blood started dripping down the well. As if some kid with a cut gum was measuring spit.

The body was like a toilet roll. All in one piece, but riddled with holes. David used his foot to turn him over. 'Is he the one?'

'I don't know.' One dwarf looks much like another.

David went through his pockets. An invitation to a dance. Two pounds seventy. A hanky. A watch. A picture of two dwarfs. Two dwarfs? Must be his brother or something. God, this is a good year for bloody dwarfs. Finally a radiation bullet. 'Must have something to do with Homer.'

That wasn't the worst of it. The really sick thing is that Homer knew we'd kill him. The bullet was a calling card, there were no arabs in the rifle. He'd sent this little guy out to be killed. And the little guy must have been so scared – he'd gone. God, that seemed worse than just killing him.

Also, the cold acknowledgement came to me, as I thought of Mel and Ron and the kid on the cart, no one was safe any more. We were running out of places to stay and people to know.

Remembering Ron, David kicked the dwarf's miserable face so hard that half the skin tore away and all his rotten teeth peeked out. Then he ran downstairs.

I threw up in a corner, then followed him. We wrestled the hysterical Mel into the cart, put Ron beside her so she could look after him – that calmed her down a bit; it was hot so she had to keep the mosquitoes and flies away from the sticky blood – picked up the shafts, and with Jaz pushing behind, headed for the hospital as fast as our six legs could take us. We didn't spare ourselves. We ran like the clappers.

But halfway there, Mel said, 'This boy's stopped breathing Barty. I think he's dead.'

TEN

Let me attempt to define my feelings during those next few days and weeks when all the terrors of the past were crowding in on me. It seemed my lot had not distilled at all.

Sick, I was. Glum as the condemned man told his reprieve was only an administrative cock-up. It seemed that I'd revised the year, but the nightmare was still the same. The nightmare that is Homer.

Utterly abject, I watched my lousy nails retreat ever further up my fingers. I couldn't retreat from the past. I couldn't escape it, evade it, delude it, suborn it with my ruined nerves. I couldn't forget it.

Pissed off, to the nth degree. Why has Fate got it in for me? What have I done to offend the world? Is it because I'm basically such a nice guy? I don't know.

It is all going so quickly. My life is flooding past. Everybody is dying or fleeing and it's all my fault. I have enough guilt at the best of times. Right now I'm crippled with it. I think it's a kind of cancer.

I must hold on to the dream. I still have to get to America. I have to find Harry, find Rachel – then we buy a passage on one of the boats and leave this nightmare and this misery behind. Why don't any good things ever happen? I can't remember the last time I had a laugh. Even my clothes don't fit me properly. The whole shape of my body seems to be altering. I need a break, a holiday, a reincarnation.

What I need is a bit of peace and quiet. And a lot of unfamiliar faces. What I don't need, is another visit from the past. The past is done, let me just try to survive in the present. Peace and quiet, that's what I need.

A voice close at heel. 'Hello cully.'

Oh my God! My entire body slumped like an emptied bladder, then contracted. I don't believe this! I turned round with suicide in my heart and started whispering through my prayers.

'Remember me, cully?' crooned an Irish voice.

I tried to nod, but my muscles had seized up. He could probably tell I remembered him though, because I started choking. Tommy, the Irish hoodlum. The guy I'd stolen two hundred grand from. On a list of folk I didn't want to meet, only Homer kept him from first place.

'Are yez pleased to see me, cully?'

I choked. 'Hu – hu – hu. . . .' I couldn't get any more than that out. I'd only come out with David to do a bit of shopping. My eyes darted round for him. I hope to God you can see me David. I hope you've got this bastard covered. If he sneezes, blast him. Trouble is, I couldn't see my saviour anywhere.

I had to do something. I had to stall until David showed. I had to keep in the open. 'You've, er, put on a bit of weight, Tommy.'

He looked puzzled. 'Have I? Not like you, eh bucko? Sure you look like you've been squeezed out the cat's bum.' Aye, and you're the one who stuffed me up there you psychopathic little leprechaun. 'Don't look so scared cully, no one's going to eat yez. Sure I've been wanting to have a talk with you for a while.'

Have you? I haven't wanted to talk with you. Well, only through a spirit-medium. 'I, er – I'm sorry about

77

the money Tommy. Something just came over me. I've still got it, you can have it back.'

'Ach! What's money boy, what's money, eh? Plenty of time for that, plenty of time.' That was one of the things that was worrying me most. His soft voice had a patient quality to it. I shuddered. 'Are you cold laddy? You're shivering.'

I shook my head. 'Just terror, you know.' I gave a hysterical and abrupt laugh.

Tommy laughed too. He liked a laugh, did Tommy. His little white face lit up like a block of ice when he smiled. His tiny tongue flicked in a lizardly fashion, in and out of his grey lips.

I wasn't the only one to shun his company. Most of the hair in the centre of his head had followed the example. He must have noticed me glance at it. He spat on his palm, smoothed a few long strands across. They looked like cracks on an egg.

'We can't talk out here, cully. Let's go in the pub and yez can buy me a jar.' Thanks very much Tommy. 'Don't worry about your little pooftah friend. One of my boys'll have a word with him.'

Tommy, only half my size, gripped me by an elbow and steered me into an establishment so select it didn't even seem to have a name. Maybe that's because most of the letters had dropped off.

At his insistence, I gave Tommy some cash and he got the drinks in. 'What'll you have, Bidet?'

'Beekay. Er, bitter please.'

He bought me a Guinness to complement his own. Pocketed my change. 'Have you got any coins for the machine, boyo, I'll get us some smokes.'

We sat down in a corner at a tiny round table littered with fag ash and scratched graffiti. I jumped up to swap my stool for one that didn't collapse when I leaned back on it.

The pub was just about deserted. A cheerless place. The barman looked like he'd been specially exhumed for the day. The hooker at the end of the bar was so myopic she lit the end of her nose twice, instead of her fag. Half an hour later, as we were leaving, she toppled off the stool, pissed. She was so myopic it's a wonder she could find the floor.

A pair of rough types were growling at another table. Sunlight was trying to push a way past the dust and the patched-up windows. There was a stuffed rat or something above the bar.

Tommy ignited our cigarettes and ran a finger around the neck of his green sports shirt. 'Hot, hey?' I nodded, tried to stop the drink slopping out of my glass. He took his old fawn raincoat off, folded it on a stool. His restless eyes explored the room.

'Someone has started killing my men off,' he said suddenly. 'Someone has hired an assassin.'

'It's not me.'

'Ach, I know it's not you,' he said scornfully. 'Sure 'tis someone who knows what they're bloody doing. They've killed eleven of my men now. Eleven good men, shot to death or blown to pieces. No I know it's not you. I know who it is. It's that bastard albino.'

'Homer?'

'Aye. The one you should have shot when you had the chance!' he said bitterly. 'That fuckin' Homer!' He stubbed his cigarette out on the table top and I drew away from the ferocious coldness of his hatred. 'That fucking cunt!' Just the look on his face made me wince.

I finished my drink with an effort and went to buy some more.

Tommy was too screwed up with his emotion to say anything more for a while. He looked at times as though he was about to cry. I hoped he'd get so upset he'd have a heart attack and I could vamoose.

'He's got to pay, cully!' he said at last. 'The bastard's got to pay!'

I kept silent. Once again I had no idea what was going on. People are a complete mystery to me.

'It's your fault you know, cully! My men shot him to save you!' The more angry he became, the more intense became his accent. It was like being shouted at by the whole of the Irish nation. The dental plate slipped off his upper gum and he shoved it back automatically. 'You and that bloody Harry!'

'Where is Harry, do you know?'

'Of course I bloody know! I know everything about you, cully! We've been watching you for weeks!'

He returned to the blackness of his memory. 'D'you remember Moose? Big Moose? He killed him last week. Do you know what he did? He put a bomb in his lavatory and when he pulled the chain sure he blew his bloody head off!'

I glanced away to conceal an involuntary smile. I don't think Tommy was relating the tale as a joke.

'He didn't even have a chance to pull his bloody trousers up! That man's sick, cully. He doesn't just kill people, he – humiliates them!' He was deadly serious and I knew exactly what he meant. 'He could go through the lot of us!' I knew that too. Homer is a pestilence. He's a vampire of lives. Death, his own imperium, is the only antivenin.

'What I want you to do boy, is to find this albino for me.'

I didn't spit my drink out, but some of it did snort

down my nostrils. I wiped my face on my sleeve and tried to think of a way to tell him to frig off without offending him.

'You've got a good little squad, cully. A four-man team. Good number.'

'Three,' I squeaked.

'Oh, I hadn't heard that. The fairy princess? Never mind, three's even better.'

'We were, er, thinking more along the lines of, er – running.'

'Aye, you would be, you little fart.' Now that was uncalled for wasn't it? 'But look at it another way. See, if you don't do it laddy, we won't kill you. We'll kill the girl.' He let that sink in. 'We'll break pieces off you, but we won't kill you.'

Hmm. A persuasive argument. It sank in a long way. I felt my guts contract, and my eyes were trying to wring out tears. I'm bloody hopeless at poker. 'We might kill you,' he added slowly. 'But only if we feel sorry for you.'

I was in a tiny room, with David, Tommy, a half-caste Irishman called Peter, a little Irish terrier of a man called Donnegan and a fellow Londoner by the name of Eric.

Of all of them, I liked the look of Eric the least. His face had the aspect of a cat that's been poisoned. His body seemed to be bursting to commit destruction, as muscular as a bronze statue. He had the worst halitosis I've ever gagged on. He smelt like he ate guano sandwiches.

Donnegan seemed all right, if you like lunatics. He kept bouncing up because he thought there was someone at the door, and there never was. He seemed to be made of wire, going rusty at the top.

Peter had the appearance of a gypsy. Hard as nails. I'll bet he has a gold loop through his penis.

It was a battle meeting. We're going to raid an army camp.

I think I've got an ulcer coming. I get through more Milk of Magnesia than a hooker does Durex. It's okay for the stomach but I spend half the day on the bog. Raid an army camp. They're out of their frigging minds.

ELEVEN

Somewhere to the south of London, a shallow river runs between gentle banks, watched by solemn files of shoulder-to-shoulder trees. If the trees have been waiting for something exciting to happen, they must have displayed unparalleled patience for some of them have died from their vigil. Some have hung their heads in their weariness. Still others have descended to cool their aching feet. Others have slouched chummily against neighbours for support. Some, the brazen ones, have stripped off their leaves and cavort naked!

The water though, doesn't care. The water does not give a toss. It grumbles past, muttering and cussing and drowning bugs. It's always in a hurry, no time to spare on entertaining stupid trees. No, the water couldn't give a toss.

Nor could I really. I turn my back on the scene. I squint as Tommy's exhaled smoke drifts into my face.

'Quite a nice spot here isn't it, cully?' he murmurs. I nod as I unbutton my fly for a nervous slash. Evening is thick.

'Kind of – romantic like.' My urine hissing into a bed of nettles sounds very romantic. 'Mind them things don't sting you.' He moves away. He doesn't like me. He thinks I'm a little fart.

I wish I was doing something else.

I'm not in very good shape. For three weeks now I've been sleeping like a nervous cat, waking up at every slightest sound. Moving to a different bed every night, trying to evade the phantom that is Homer, is not good for your piss and vinegar. My nerves are so bad at the moment that if a joint in my leg cracks my heart stops.

I don't seem to have had a decent night's sleep – since I was about ten. Then someone told me about things that go bump in the night and I've been hearing them ever since. Things that go bump in the day worry me enough. When I'm not sitting up worrying about Homer, I'm having nightmares about the Canal.

Every one of us is frightened of the albino. You can see the strain on all our faces. Like a dark and pallid disease. Look at mine, I give all the appearance of being a rehearsal for a cadaver.

My new image didn't last long. I've given up the clean-shaven look. Couldn't stand all the scratches and burst pimples. My hair is starting to get long again, ducks'-bums and kiss-curls all over the place. My clothes are getting frayed. Clothes just fall apart when they get on me, I'm not kidding. It must be something in my sweat.

It's bloody hot this evening. Even the midges are troubled by midges. They don't bother me too much though. Probably frightened they'll catch something. Tommy's going crazy, slapping at his face like an insane percussionist.

Let's hear it for the midges!

I creep back to Jaz and David. They're very quiet. David has been quiet since Ron died a month ago, full of grief. If he was a woman, I could maybe console him. But I don't know what to say to David. I'm frightened he'll start crying.

Jaz is just quiet. She always is.

She's let her hair grow long too, wears it in a ponytail. She only looks about fourteen. A tiny gamine of a girl. She has a dress on for the dido tonight. A green one, with a flouncy skirt. And high-heels.

'It's a long way round to get at Homer,' David murmurs.

I nod.

'And even if we get him, these Irishmen will kill us.'

I nod again.

'Or the Pox. Or somebody.'

Tired of nodding I simply stare.

'It's not the glorious game I thought it was,' David went on.

'You don't have to hang around you know. You can go.' I would, if I thought I'd get away.

He shrugged. 'Don't know what else to do. I don't want to die though.'

'If we get Homer, we'll probably live longer.'

'And what about the Irish?'

'You're in a bloody cheerful mood tonight!' As a comforter, I'm bloody useless. On a scale of one to ten – oh forget it.

Jaz chipped in. 'It's better than being in prison!'

David nodded. 'I'd just rather we were on our way to America.'

It's the only thing that keeps us all going. We sat there glum as trolls.

Two o'clock. The moon is high.

Unlike my spirits; they've notched up a new low.

Hiding in the trees, the air is spectral and devilishly clear. I can hear the hairs in my nose rustling in my breath. Almost. Tommy taps me on the shoulder. 'All right, send her now.'

I croak a whisper to Jasmine. She pinches my bum and sets off, pushing a pram. She doesn't seem as scared as me. Perhaps it's her youth. Perhaps it's my pusillanimity.

She clambers up the little bank on to the road, wheels the creaking pram towards the training-camp entrance. I can't bear to look, I close my eyes. Yes I can, they snap open again. 'If she fucks this up cully, I'll cut your eyeballs out.'

Jaz nears the gate, where the outer sentry sits in his little box about ten yards from the road. We can see him through the glasses. He looks to be reading a mag. Military discipline is going all to hell.

The air is as still as the water in a font. No sound to distract but the insects. We hear every click of the wonky back wheel, every creak of the rusting body. Jasmine's heels tap unevenly, click plop, click plop. She pauses at the mouth of the roadlet leading into the sleeping camp.

For a long moment she waits, a childlike revenant in the ghastly light of silvery lamps. Two lamps, one is steady and bright, the other flickers redly like the silver heart has been cut. For a long moment, she hesitates.

But then her tiny head turns, and we catch her voice, louder than a whisper, softer than a cry. 'Excuse me!'

The sentry stirs, peers suspiciously through his cracked pane. 'Excuse me . . .' Trailing the pram Jasmine steps towards the box.

'Yeah, worrayawan'?' The young soldier steps outside, wiping his mouth. His white cap is pushed to the back of his head. His jacket is at a sloppy angle. Jasmine levels her gun, holding it two-handed. Straight at his eyes. The sentry freezes.

'Right, she's got him,' says Tommy. 'Let's go!'

We start forward. But the sentry makes a wrong move. Jasmine fires. The gun is silenced. There's a dunk! The geezer staggers back with a fountain coming from his heart. He throws himself on to his back and lies still.

'Oh God Jesus, cully, she's shot the bastard!'

We spill forward, myself bringing up the rear. A dozen bums in front of me wobble up the bank. One pumps.

Men race to the gate, a sniper's rifle pokes through the metal mesh. The inner sentry steps from his cabin to check the commotion. Dunk dunk! All the colour rushes to his face. There's suddenly a space where he was standing.

A rattle as someone clears the gate. The biggest wire cutters I've ever seen jaw at stubborn chains. The gate rattles back. Our band pushes forward. One at the gate, already slipping into the dead man's bloody coat.

Jasmine pushes me away. Throws the pram behind a bush. Follows the others. I run, catch up with Tommy.

We slip past sleeping huts, creeping through darkness like wraiths. Figures peel off, taking up positions of observation. Keeping a route to the gate open. I hope.

A dog barks beyond the perimeter. All I can hear is breathing, the occasional mutter of stones under feet. I'm too tense to be truly afraid. It's more like a naughty game. Of course nobody's shooting at us yet.

We skirt the drilling ground, past the flagpole with its furled flag. The camp sleeps on like it's drugged. Just another night. Not an eyelid flickers. David appears at my side, taps me nervously. Or maybe I just ran into him. He drops at the last corner, covers our backs to the stone-built armoury. Metal shutters cover the small windows. Huge metal doors.

I crouch down with Tommy and the insane Donnegan. The lunatic sets to work on the three locks like a dentist. His slim tools clink and scrape. I pop another hay fever tab.

Five minutes pass. The door is still closed. Donnegan is murmuring. We should be out of here by now.

'I thought he was a fucking locksmith,' I mutter to Tommy.

'Do you want to fucking do it?' I shut up, try to reassure my heart which is hammering like a demented bird at the bars of its cage.

Three minutes agonize by. Donnegan grouses more fiercely. 'This shitey, goddamned – fuckin' bloody . . .'

I turn away, thinking I hear a sound. But it's nothing.

The locks are like desperate virgins. They cling on grimly to what they've got. Donnegan doesn't turn them on at all. He can't even get past their overcoats. Tommy is breathing ever more heavily. My body remembers that it hasn't trembled for a while and breaks out all over. I'm drenched in a cool sweat.

'What's the fucking matter with you, Donnegan?' hisses Tommy.

'Don't blame me! It's not me, it's these fucking locks!'

I wandered to the corner, looked about. It was like a night on the ocean. Nothing but shhh. Where the hell is Jasmine? I hope she's stuck with David.

Actually, I've never spent a night on the ocean. I've never spent a night anywhere but on dry land. Except when I've been crocko. Then I've been a bit tidal.

I heard a clicking kind of noise, which I thought might be bats. But it turned out to be wax in my ears. Nobody seemed to be stirring though. The only sonance was Donnegan's escalating temper. I was beginning to doubt that he'd ever seen a bloody lock before, let alone picked one. Natural erosion could do the job quicker than him.

A lot of stars, giving me the eye. Half a moon. I wonder who nicked the other half?

I wonder whatever happened to the space shuttle? I suppose they just ran out of money. Old shuttles never die. They just fade out of the budget.

Do you believe in sixth sense? Well I'm a good example of someone who doesn't have it. I'm not sure that I've got the normal five actually. But when the first sign of something going wrong occurred, it took me completely by surprise.

Well it didn't surprise me in the sense that I'm ever expecting things to go wrong. It's just that it had been so quiet for the last few minutes, I wasn't anticipating anything just then.

I came back to earth with a jolt. 'What was that?' hissed Tommy.

Somebody shouted. There was a pattering of running feet. I pressed into the wall.

Another shout. Over the far side of the compound. Then more feet. A general sense of confusion. Of foreboding. A light flickered, a torch maybe. That dog barked again. A couple of lights came on.

'What the hell's going on?'

'I don't know.'

Then somebody fired a gun.

The gunshot drew out more lights.

More gunshots.

Shouting.

'Oh come on Donnegan, out the fucking way! I'll shoot the bastards off!'

I turned round. 'No – this'll do it.' I put a grenade

down by the metal doors, pulled the pin. It was like playing with fireworks. 'Beat it!' They'd already gone.

I scarpered myself. Jumped over a low wall, stuck my fingers in my ears. Clenched my bum. Get ready David, this will attract some attention!

The bang made my sinuses pop. I scrambled up a bit dazed, scampered back to the door. Oh bloody hell, the metal was all twisted and buckled but it was still pretty much in place. There was just about room to squeeze down the side. If you didn't have an erection. It was bloody awkward though. And dangerous – that metal hadn't split into gentle curves. 'Tommy? Tommy?'

Some people ran along the side of the building towards me. But they sounded more hostile than the little Irishman. I dived for cover, made sure my automatic pistol was aware of the situation.

They ran past. Four big feet. I peered out cautiously, straining into the gloom. It was all clear. But where the hell was everybody? There was a lot of screaming and banging some way off. I risked a shout. 'David?'

'Yes?'

'Are you okay?'

'Yes.'

'Do you know where Jaz is?'

'She's right here.'

'I'm right here!'

I went back to the door, pulled half-heartedly at the handles. I span around. What the hell is *that*? It sounds like a JCB masturbating. The ground shuddered right behind me. A light came on.

Oh my God it's a tank! I dropped the gun like it had just farted, threw my hands in the air.

Then Tommy's head poked out of the top. 'Will yez

90

get out of the bleedin' way you bastard, I want to knock the flamin' doors down!'

I looked around wildly. I think I was on the brink of hysteria. Then I hopped out of the way. I couldn't believe it. David came running up. 'What's going on?'

I couldn't speak. I just waved my arms at the advancing tank. 'Who's in that?'

I still couldn't speak. Finally a few words ungummed themselves and blurted out, 'That fucking Irishman!'

The doors buckled inwards with the squeal of a thousand virgins, collapsed with a bang. Tommy clambered down, a squirrel with diarrhoea. Donnegan appeared.

'Come on, cully! Get some of the bloody stuff out!' He was pretty tense. He was screaming through his teeth. I followed the torchlights inside.

We bundled out crates of grenades, detonators, bazookas, shells, mines. 'Come on cully, come on!' Bullets followed, a couple of mortars. We worked liked demons, like slaves on inspection day.

'Put it up on the tank! Pass it in to me!'

I scrambled up with Donnegan, started passing the stuff in. Sweat was cascading off me. My armpits were waterfalls. 'You can't steal a fucking tank!' I said. But nobody listened.

Donnegan disappeared somewhere. The tank started to roar. 'Hold on, cully! We're getting out of here!'

I peered down into the gloomy hatch. I could see the top of Tommy's head and one of his legs. We lurched back a couple of yards, like the tank was retching.

'You can't steal a frigging tank!' I screamed. I kept on shouting it. But he was too stupid to listen. He just kept laughing like an idiot and slapping his thigh.

'We're going backwards! We're going to hit that bleeding wall!'

But it didn't make any difference. We just went straight through it.

There was a thump and Jasmine appeared, clinging on beside me. 'Are we stealing this?'

'Don't you start!'

We were in the lane now and people were shooting at us. Tommy swung away, through the trees, down towards the river. Branches were whipping at our faces like masochists at the hunt-ball.

We splashed into the river. My bones were juddering like skeletons on jack-hammers. Every tooth in my body was being crushed.

'The Brits taught me this you know, cully! I was in the army for them! Out in Norway!'

Give the moron credit, we did seem to be actually getting away with it. The major battle that appeared to have taken over the army camp was definitely receding. It sounded as though some of the Irish had taken refuge in the armoury. That should keep everyone busy for a while.

But what were we getting away to?

And, more important at that moment, what the hell had happened to David? Why wasn't he with us?

I let go with one hand to wipe the sweat out of my eyes.

BOOK TWO

ONE

I was near the point where I could get into trouble deep. Like so deep you'd never see me come up again.

Thomas the Irish wanted me to infiltrate one of the big London street gangs, the squads, which he thought had some connection with Homer. It seems the albino is on a personal crusade. He's been kicked out of the army.

I was either to sniff the psycho out or act as bait. Like thanks a bunch, Tommo. Whoopee.

That was why all the weaponry had been stolen. It was to be used to chaffer my way in. Tommy didn't think I had much else to offer. He reckoned my 'reputation' would last until the first time someone spat or farted near me, at which point I'd probably burst into tears. He's probably right. So the hardware was meant to compensate for that. And also the news of the haul would hopefully bring Homer, long before my true nature uncovered itself. I say 'hopefully' with a certain sarcasm.

A bloody expensive subscription though, as five of the guys didn't make it back to the rendezvous. One of whom was David. Another score to settle. Some time. Somehow. These guys don't count the cost in those terms though. To them, it's what you gain, not what you lose.

So I'm left garnering all these grudges the way other people collect stamps. And then left wondering what the hell to do with them. Where does one go to cash the damn things in? It's best just to be phlegmatic. Which I can't be.

Anyway, I didn't fancy my kamikaze role at all. Not one little bit. Even less than that. If Homer didn't get me, Tommy and his false teeth sure as hell would. Not only that, it was taking me further and further away from where I wanted to be. I mean, I'm not interested in bloody revenge; I don't want to turn the streets of London into a hunting ground. All I want to do is get my friends together, get our money dug up and get us all across to America where maybe we've got a chance to lead a decent sort of life. All this fighting from day to day and living for the next fear, is no good at all. So first chance I got, I grabbed hold of Jaz and we buggered off.

You can't fight someone like Homer. You can't track him down like it's some cheap detective novel. We're just a bunch of amateurs. Homer's top of the league. Even Tommy and his battle-hardened boys, they're sitting ducks for someone like that. The guy eats death for breakfast.

Our best chance of escaping him was to put the Atlantic Ocean between us. Without David I had no bloody chance of gunning the guy.

I just keep hoping he'll contract some terrible disease. But the people you really despise never do. They're like those old musicals they drag up out of the vaults. They just go on and on. And on.

It's not easy though to lead a life divorced from life. For a start, we were getting low on cash. Down to our last eight quid and a fifty-pence-off coupon. So I tried to hold up an off-licence.

The guy just laughed, told me to piss off. I suppose I should have at least bandied words with him, but scenes really aren't my scene. So instead I tried to burgle a house, but I couldn't get the flaming window open. God, half the morons in the country do it – what's wrong with me?

In the end, while I was still debating what to do next, Jasmine disappeared for an hour and came back with thirty quid.

What could I do? I don't own the girl. It bought us a bed for the night and something to eat. I thought I wouldn't be able to sleep for guilt but I went out like a light. Can't even rely on your own conscience. Do you think I'm becoming harder? Maybe Mel was right, maybe I am more cynical. Or maybe I was just tired.

We spent the next day sitting in a park, trying to figure out a next move. Jaz conned a couple of ice creams. I had to fight a wasp for mine. Bloody things. They have a nose for stark terror. In the end I caught the bugger with a left jab and it soared off.

That gave everyone around a good laugh. That's me, good for a laugh. I scowled round at them all. That wiped it off their greasy pans. Ha ha. 'You're a miserable bastard,' said Jasmine.

'Did I ask you how I should look at people? Did I?' Life's bad enough without being put right.

'Your face won't crack you know.'

It might. I'm frightened that if I remove the scowl I'll burst into tears. Sometimes, the way my teeth ache, I think it's only the grimace that holds them in place. That and plaque.

You know, life is bloody weird at the moment. I don't seem to be making any progress at all with mine. I'm not even treading water. I'm what? twenty-eight. I've got no future, a lousy history, and the here and now stinks. I'd be better off if I was a germ. At least they have some purpose in life. I wouldn't mind spreading disease.

This idle reverie's a waste of time. I'm just delaying a decision. Can't spend the rest of our lives sitting in a bloody park. You get raped in parks when the lights go out. I know, my mother told me.

Got to get myself organized. Got to figure out some proper kind of plan, we're not going to get anywhere like this. There must be some way I can sort things out, I'm not stupid. Trouble is, it seems such a big bloody country. So many things to do and I don't even know where to start looking.

Oh come on Beak, think for chrissake! Why is my brain suddenly so feeble and useless? I think maybe senile dementia has set in. Maybe I've got some degenerative brain disease. Seem to have lost the power of rational thought. Not that I had a lot of it to start with.

Oh hell, what are we going to do? Nothing but bad news.

The authorities want me. The army wants me. A bald psychopath wants me. Irish terrorists want me. Them aside, the rest of the world is doing its best to ignore me. How the hell am I going to sort out my mess from the middle of all that lot? God, America seems a million miles away.

Christ, I can't even picture tomorrow.

Jaz got hold of some more money and we took a really low dive down Bermondsey way. The Land of Darkness. A tenny so low it couldn't raise itself to even look at a scale of one to ten. I mean, I've been in some shite-awful places, but nothing this bad. It's a place you can only live in if you keep your eyes shut and don't touch anything.

God, and I had such high hopes for myself.

It is truly a sick house. All its skin is flaking away. Its nose keeps running. Most of the windows need glasses. Christ knows what's wrong with the doors, but you only have to look at them and they fall off. They don't hang even approximately vertically. The guy who put them up must have been in a strait-jacket.

There's a smell I won't even attempt to describe. The water comes out grey – if it comes. And the bog has a habit of vomiting back at you every time you flush it. Which you have to do with a bucket of water cos there's no bleeding cistern. And I seem to be the only one in the bloody house who bothers. Some people use the sink.

You can't even shut the door properly. All sorts of looney people stroll in to watch while you're trying to relieve your constipation.

Have you ever read anything by that old guy, Borges? He wrote some pretty good stuff. There was one piece, he was writing about someone who'd died, and said something like 'like all men, he was given bad times in which to live.' They couldn't have been as bad as these.

It's an immigrant house. We're the only white ones in here. Except for a couple of Jews downstairs and a young chick who lackeys for one of the black guys. She isn't all there. She isn't even halfway there.

Jews and coloureds, they're the poor buggers who have to live in places like this. Jews and coloureds and me and Jaz.

It's all these bloody fascists, going round stirring everybody up. They'll take over this country the way they're going on. They had a big march through London the other day and they got nearly a million people. A million people! It's bloody incredible.

That's nearly as many people as use this bloody toilet.

Fascists. They wanted me to join up a couple of years ago. But I ran away before they could beat me up. They're usually too busy to explain why you should be a fascist. So they just show you what it will be like if you're not.

Of course if you sign up with the fascists the bloody communists come round and beat the crap out of you! If someone comes up with an extreme right-wing communist group, maybe I'll join. All I know is – not knowing too much about politics – there are bad guys and even worse guys. And you can bet your fanny if there's any screwing going on, I'll be on the end of it.

What I need is a party of the uncommitted. A party of don't knows and don't-want-to-knows. I'd probably do all right in a group like that. Be a damn sight better than the fascists, with all their marching up and down and shouting and polishing their boots with ox-blood and meeting at the pub every Thursday. They don't half like shouting.

People say to me, 'What would the world be like if everybody had your attitude?' And then they walk off and get beaten up or mugged or raped or something. They're out of their bloody minds!

I remember we had a mock election once at school. I put my vote down for the Receiving Officer. But I was too frightened to own up to it. Another time I said I wanted to withhold my vote on principle, because I didn't like any of the buggers, and the teacher put a cross down for me. He said I was an anarchist. He was

100

just annoyed because I told him he kept spelling 'election' wrong. He used a 'k'.

That's about the limit of my involvement with politics. Having my vote cast for me. That kind of sums me up.

I have to confess, I like the fascists least of all. I'm always frightened they're going to start picking on skinny guys with bad skin and hay fever. That Fitzwilliam, he was a fascist. Even Tommy didn't like him. Even I didn't like him, and I'm a very tolerant guy.

Mind you, they might be fascists, but have they actually murdered anyone? I have. Once you start getting into morality you really start poking your toe up your nose. You might as well hallucinate that you're God.

The house we're in is the sort of establishment fascists head for when they've had a few. We live in a top room. We keep the blind down so that Homer can't see us. In fact we don't even go near the window. Which is a bit awkward in a small room. We spend most of our time limbo dancing past it.

We've got a little radio and we play cards a lot. We don't have much to cook on, just a little gas ring. But we don't have much to cook anyway. Sometimes we play hunt the roach. There are so many of them though you don't have to look far.

It's mucky. So are we. Can't be bothered fetching water. The tap's downstairs, out the back. We have to wash in the bucket.

We don't laugh a lot. You wouldn't like to be invited round for an evening. Nor would I.

I tell Jaz to go out and get herself a boyfriend. But she says she doesn't like boys. A prostitute who doesn't like boys. What's the world coming to? Maybe all hookers dislike their clients. I don't know.

That's what she's becoming, a prostitute. I suppose that makes me a pimp. I wish she had some family to go to. But she knows less people than me.

I'm not the sort of person she should hang about with. She'll get shot or arrested or something. I like her well enough. She gets a bit of a bore sometimes. Particularly when she keeps winning at cards. I owed her about eight million smackers at the last count.

The people downstairs are weird. The Jews. They're what you would call – nice people. Incredibly nice people in fact. Always trying to give you things. Bits of food, cheese and stuff like that. First couple of times I thought it must be poisoned – you get like that these days – so I fed it to a dog.

I've never met any nice people before. I'm more used to dealing with bastards and dildoes.

His wife's a sick woman though. Mrs Grossman. I don't know what's wrong with her but it's eating her up like acid. I've only known her a couple of weeks; but she crinkles up even as you watch her. She's also asthmatic.

Mr Grossman used to work in the sewers. Until one collapsed on him. He's half crippled.

We've started eating a lot of meals at the canteen now. You can sneak an odd one now and again; but to do it regularly you need one of the green cards. Jasmine managed to procure us a couple. We could hardly go and register at the post office, could we?

There was a really bad fight there yesterday. Nearly a goddamned riot.

There are always fights at the welfare canteens. The Bins. Someone coughs on someone's plate; someone

102

slops someone's tea; someone's got the wrong brand of sweat on. There's a fight. I once saw a bozo slash someone's nose off with a razor because he got the last of the sausages.

I heard tell, that in a fight at one Bin on the north side, someone was spiked in the gut and threw up. And some kid ate it! People are goddamn animals, do you know that? They're worse than animals.

The goddamn places are designed for trouble anyway. What they do is say, open a Bin to cater for two thousand people, and then send enough food for seventeen hundred. There's probably meant to be food for two grand. It's just someone's getting fat. And it ain't the binnies.

The food they serve you they must get from taxidermists. It tastes like recycled sewage. On a day all the machines are off. Bad? Would I kid you? On a scale of one to ten, it's minus twelve. You wouldn't use it to polish your boots. If it came out of your bum you'd go to the doc's.

When you've got them hungry enough though, they'll eat shit. If they served out chopped up people, they'd fight for seconds.

The people who go to the Bins are pretty low in the totem of humanity. If life was a church, they'd be the bugs that feed on the dung in the belfry. Me and Jaz, we queue right along with them.

I can't stand it. Sometimes I think I'm going to scream. Sometimes, I'm sick into my mouth and have to force it down again. It makes me want to cry. But I don't know what else to do. I can't stand being hungry. My weight must be down to about nine stone. And I'm over six foot.

We try to get against a wall out of the way. You can

103

see any trouble coming then. There are two types to watch out for. Men, and women. If you get a table to yourself you might be okay. But wheresoever three or more gather together, trouble hovers overhead like a Valkyrie.

Yesterday we were at adjoining tables with our dorsals against a square green pillar. The place was chocker. It was steaming. The air outside was blistering in the heat. The meal was curried mince.

We didn't say anything, kept our faces down to our plates, chewed on grimly. The usual hubbub washed back and forth like a slopping tide. The *brouhaha* of the Bin.

Do you remember that bit of a poem that Hangerman wrote about Junk City? Well he did one on the Bins. 'Ode on the State Welfare Canteens' it was called. Classy title huh? One piece went:

The food in the Bins isn't fit for a pig.
But the people who eat it don't give a frig, d'you dig?

Personally I find him a little dated. As well as appalling. God knows how he got to be Poet Laureate.

Sweat was plopping off us. Plopping off everybody. The corridor where you have to queue up was like a dog's tongue. You could put it through a sieve.

Then somebody tripped, a young dame. She paid a heavy mulct for her carelessness. Her bowl of mince went straight over some big joe with a face like a cabbage. He yelled like a kick in the haemorrhoids.

Next moment the chick's on her back with the gazebo's boot chiselling into her face. She didn't cry out, there were no openings left to cry from. Her features were just a pulp. But she thrashed a lot.

A second doxy flung herself across the table and

104

caught the big guy through the throat with a fork. She didn't let it go, she wrenched it backwards and forwards under his chin. There was more blood than the day the tomato soup urn broke the table. You could see her sticking it in deeper and deeper, right up to her fist. It must have been through the bottom of his mouth, skewering his tongue.

He elbowed her in the tits, grabbed a knife and as she sprawled on the table he smashed it down through her eye and left it there, sticking out like the prosthetic work of a madman. She must have died pretty quick, it looked to have gone a couple of inches into her brain. She was a weeping corpse, twitching off the table before anyone really saw her face. I think she had red hair.

By this time me and Jaz were off the seats and edging away. Jaz nimmed a couple of lumps of bread while heads were turned.

There was a moment's pause as though that might be the end of it. Then all of a sudden a metal table leg appeared in the middle of big joe's head, splitting it down the middle. He fell back, his chums jumped up, a bunch of skins fell on them, and the next second the whole place is going berserk. It was like the devils had found the door of hell.

There must have been four hundred people, slashing the guts out of one another. A little kid was picked up and just thrown through a window. We were on the second floor.

Then someone started smashing all the windows and skimming chunks of glass across the room. One almost took off the hairs in my nostrils. Thank God I was inhaling at the time. But lots of people caught them in the face. Fortunately someone kicked the bastard out.

She didn't stop screaming even when she was lying in the street with a broken back. Alongside the little kid who'd landed head first on an old parking meter post. He was dead. They'd have to slide him off.

Someone set fire to the oil in the kitchen and started slinging that about. People love a chance to hurt each other. It was like the World Screaming Championship.

We couldn't get to the door. We crouched under a table in the farthest corner of the room. All the grey paint was being flecked with red.

We crawled to the nearest window. But it was thirty feet to the pavement. We saw the first dingoes arrive. A busload. They bundled out, whipping their wands from their back pockets, checking their guns were secure. A lot of dogs get shot with their own bang-bangs.

Now it was really going to get nasty.

Dragging a table with us for protection, we made it to the fire doors. The cavalry could sort it out. And afterwards they'd probably check everyone. Which meant us. And I don't even look remotely like the bozo on my green card. We kicked the door open and buggered off.

TWO

Things took off again with a sudden spurt.

The year had jerked its way as far as the balmy month of August. Nearly my birthday. Time to worry again about getting old. About whether I'll die of old age or whether Homer will cut me short.

Ah, what's the point in worrying though, what's the difference? Die today, die tomorrow. It's all the same.

But it isn't. I don't want to die, today, tomorrow, for ever.

By the same token, I guess I don't fancy living much. It's hardly a day-by-day exploration of the deeper reaches of Joy. But even when the living's tough, you don't know that death isn't a goddamn sight worse. Living might be bloody fantastic compared with death. Even eating in the Bins, nightmaring about colossal bald albinoes. If there's a hell, Homer will certainly be there. Stalking the catacombs. Lurking in dark corners.

I wonder what the guy was like when he was a kid. I could have played gutter games with him. Well, probably not, I don't remember playing with anyone when I was a kid, too busy being surly. But you know what I mean.

I think I'm getting older. I'm not as hysterical as I used to be.

Came back from the river today. Been down there

throwing lumps of tarmac at the rats. It's something to do.

Mr Grossman's in the street in his underpants and shirt. Crying. Everyone's laughing at him. He's pushing sixty. 'What's the matter Mr Grossman?'

'Oh Bartholomew, Bartholomew –' that's me by the way, in case you forgot '– it's my wife. She collapsed. We gotta get her to the hospital. None of these schlocks will help! They just laugh!' He turned to face all their smirking, sniggering pusses and waved his arms like an old woman. 'Pigs! Pigs!'

'Come on in, Mr Grossman. We'll get her to the hospital.'

He grabbed me by the arm. 'I think she's dying, Bartholomew,' he said earnestly. 'I think this time she will die.'

We hurried inside. Up the stairs past the dog shit and the vomit. There was a dead rat on the second landing, a stick through its belly.

Mrs Grossman was slumped on the kitchen floor, breathing like a knackered sparrow. 'Put your trousers on, Mr Grossman.' She smelt terrible. I couldn't go near her for a minute. Then she started to move, waving like some marine creature too long out of water. I squatted down. 'Mrs Grossman?' She just wheezed, like if I watched her much longer I'd see her die.

Mr Grossman staggered through the door, stumbling into his trousers which were about eight sizes too big. His wife probably told him he'd grow into them. He was still crying. His glasses were all steamed up with thumb prints.

I put my arms under Mrs Grossman's shoulders and legs. Trying to avoid the muck on her thighs. I hoisted her up on to my knees. Frigging hell she was heavy. She was built like an elf. Her bones must be made of lead. 'That's it, good boy Bartholomew! Come now, quickly, quickly!'

I struggled up, hoicked her into a better position. She groaned and for a minute I thought she'd stopped breathing. But she took off again.

Mr Grossman clattered downstairs and I lumbered after. Out in the street I looked at all the gawping bastards.

'Has anyone got a pram or something?' It was two miles to the hospital. They just looked. I could have been asking for the time on Venus. 'A pram! Have you got a fucking pram one of you?' Oh shit almighty. Come on Mr Grossman. I set off as fast as I could. Mr Grossman ran by my side, sideways like a crab. His vest was on back-to-front.

I was getting lower and lower, like Groucho Marx. Someone stopped me, quite an old bloke. 'Is she dead?'

'Frig off!' I shoved him aside. Mr Grossman spat at him. Good for you Mr Grossman.

I had to keep stopping to rest her across my knees. Mr Grossman was trying to help carry her. But he held her as if she was a cracked egg. We'd never have got there. I sent him on ahead, told him to get a wheelchair or something. But he'd run on a way and then dart back. I was practically overtaking him. The poor schlep must have been breaking up. So was I. The muscles of my arms felt run through with six-inch nails. I daren't put her down, I'd never pick her up again. Needed to blow my nose; kept trying to wipe it on my shoulder.

Mrs Grossman began to dribble. It was kind of greenish. There were huge black and red thumps in the front of my skull. Great hammer blows that shook my entire brain. I'd have to run little stretches with my eyes closed; it seemed to make it easier. Relatively speaking. I knew she was going to die. I could feel it through my arms. She smelt like she was dead. It was a waste of bloody time. But I couldn't stop. Mr Grossman was already wailing.

We staggered up the ramp into the hospital and a lot of people milling about ignored us. I pushed through with Mr Grossman twittering at my heels like a faithful chick. I found some virago in a white coat filling in forms with gibberish.

'I need a doctor to see this woman. She's very ill.'

'What?' She looked at me like I was a bagful of diarrhoea.

'We need a doctor.'

'Sit down and wait your turn.' She pointed to a jungle of occupied seats.

'If we have to wait she'll be dead.'

'I can't help that. There are plenty of other people who need a doctor you know, she's not the only one.'

'If you don't get a doctor now I'll rip your frigging nose off your face!'

She didn't flinch. She must have pressed a button somewhere. All of a sudden two stubbly faces were breathing into my ears. 'You want something fartarse?'

'I want a doctor. This woman's dying.'

'They're all dying. Siddown and wait.' They had a way about them. Like the way they poked their fingers in my face. I looked at Mr Grossman helplessly. He shook his head, flicking tears. He understood.

We sat down. We waited three hours for a doctor. Mrs Grossman died on the floor between us. I still don't know what she died of. They didn't trouble to find out.

*

That was the genesis of a spate of sickness and hospitals.

When I got back with Mr Grossman, helped him into the smell of his room, Jasmine was complaining of bodily dysfunctions.

'What's the matter with you?'

'Well I had a sore, a few months ago, on me – you know. But it went after a bit so I thought it must be all right. But it's come back again now. And I've got sores in my mouth, and I'm all hot and aching. And I've got a rash.' She was a child again now. The woman she'd gained had gone with the sickness.

'A rash? What sort of rash?'

'On me chest.'

'Where's the sore?'

'On me thing – you know.'

'Your fanny?'

'Yeah.'

'It sounds like VD.'

'What's that?'

Jeez! 'An occupational hazard,' I muttered. Always right there with a witticism. Usually an old one. 'You'll have to go to the clinic.'

'They won't give me an injection will they?'

'Only if it's cheap. Otherwise they'll probably connect you to a light socket and blast it out.'

'They won't, will they?'

'No, I'm just joking.' I think.

'What'll they do then?'

'I don't know. Give you something for it.'

'Is it serious?'

'Probably not. We'll go along there tomorrow.'

'It won't hurt will it?'

111

'It'll hurt a damn sight less than if you don't go. It mightn't be anything. It might just be thrush or something.'

'Will you come with me?'

'Of course I'll come with you!' Apart from anything else, it might be catching.

THREE

A couple of days later Mr Grossman beckoned me into his quarters. He mumbled something but I didn't snare it. He rooted through a drawer bursting at its seams. His braces hung down round his knees. Barefoot. White as the bellies of fish.

I sat like a child. I sucked my lip.

He took an age, in a drawer about two foot square. I didn't say anything. I was wiped out. I hadn't been sleeping well.

The Grossmans had tried hard with the room. They'd hidden most of the damp patches. Not much they could do with the ceiling, but they'd tried to paint it, stuffed paper into the cracks. There were icons on the walls.

It was about twelve foot square. The carpet was a couple of army blankets. The furniture wasn't bad. At least it didn't fall over. Everything was brown. Even Mr Grossman's teeth which stared at me from a shelf. They were easier out than in; they were too big.

He turned round holding a pistol.

Hairs all over my body, even on my groin, horripilated. But he wasn't pointing the popper at me.

'I used to carry this with me, all the time,' he said. 'Wherever I went. Even to the . . .' he waved a hand in the direction of the pissoir.

'You should be careful of that thing, Mr Grossman. You'll get into trouble.'

113

'What, you want I should let that rabble hurt me? The fascists!' What could I say? 'One day – one day, I will kill them!' He seemed a little frail to be shouting like that.

'But you are right. A gun is not for me. Not now. Let them kill me. Already my life is –'

'You shouldn't talk like that, Mr Grossman.' Is that the right thing to say? I never know what to say. 'You've got your daughter, your sons. You don't want to give up.'

If anybody ever hung his head, Mr Grossman hung his then. 'I do want to give up. I have shame for living; shame that I should want to die.'

The terrible thought came to me that he was going to blast himself right in front of me. Felo de se in public. But he sighed and passed me the gun. For Christ's sake don't ask me to do it! 'You should have this. For luck. For protection.'

'Do you think I need protection?' He's not psychic is he?

'Today, *everyone* needs protection! Even God,' he muttered as he turned back to the drawer.

I fiddled almost automatically with the gun while Mr Grossman maundered on. I really needed a weapon. Jaz and I had fled empty-handed. That shows how much I've changed; one time I'd have run a mile from a gun. Only four slugs. It needed cleaning. It was full of lint.

'I wanted to give you something else. But now I can't find it.'

'Sorry?'

'Something else. Something else for you. I've forgotten. No matter.' He sat down on the edge of his bed like all the old men of the world, and stared at the floor.

I had a feeling Mr Grossman wasn't going to live much longer. One way or another. His quietus was approaching. He'd gone all to pieces in the last couple of days. The dirt peeled off him. It was sad. He was a nice bozo. I liked him.

I liked him less as he got dirtier.

He didn't know what to say. He was trying to find something in his brain. So was I. Some moments suit a silence. This wasn't one of them.

'Why don't you go live with one of your children, Mr Grossman?'

He shrugged. 'They don't like me much. I don't like them. You're a lonely man Bartholomew, do you know that?'

He's not going to start getting philosophical is he? 'Am I?'

He nodded. The sum of all those years inclined thoughtfully. He was like a tree in winter. No leaves. You could see the sky through the branches. 'Lonely people, they need all the help – ' He kept breaking off as though some other thought was struggling to intrude. Perhaps it wasn't a thought; perhaps it was blankness.

'Already you've got no friends. You, a young man, you got no friends. What will you be at my age?' he shouted. 'It's not just a friend for you. You can be friend to other people!'

I nodded ruminatively. What the hell is he on about?

'You know your trouble?' He was still shouting. As much for his benefit as for mine I think. It penetrated his loneliness, futility.

'You think you're very different! And you're not! I see it in your eyes, you think you're a poor man. A man betrayed! But who is the betrayer, Bartholomew, who is? You are!' He levelled a stern finger at me. I winced.

115

'There's more to life than living. You got to know you're living! You take that sick girl, and you – get the hell out of here while you can! This house – is a house for the beaten!' He paused. 'Now I remember what it was. . . .' He turned, mumbling, and rummaged through the socks in the drawer.

'Here!' He threw something at me. 'You take that! You know what that is?' It looked like a fruit-machine token. 'That's a krugerrand! Worth a lot of money! Take it and go, you and the girl. Keep out of the ghetto!'

It took me a while to locate my voice. 'I can't take this.'

'You can, you ruddy can! It was mine and I give it to you. I saved it for thirty years, forty years, now it's yours. Spend it. Buy your way up. Make a start. That's all it is, a start. A gun and the gold, it's enough!' Then he sat down on the bed and stared at the floor again.

'Mr Grossman, I can't take this. You're going to need it.'

'Shut up. I don't want to talk.'

We sat there in quietude. Well, more kind of numb in my case. There had to be something I could say that would make sense of all this. But I couldn't think what. How the hell much is a krugerrand worth?

'It's worth a lot of money.' He must be psychic. It gave me quite a start that.

'Why don't you give it to the Jewish orphanage?' It seems a lot of responsibility to me, a gift. Especially a gift that hombres would section your gullet for.

'Jews make me sick!' Fair enough. It was growing more like mine with every moment. I could feel it getting warm in my hand.

'You're not a good man, Bartholomew. That's what

116

I think. You're too much coward to be a good man. You hide behind crazy fences.' He tapped his temple. 'Crazy in the head fences!

'But you're the best there is. So take it and go. I don't want to see you again.'

'I'm –' I didn't know what to say.

'I know, I know. Everybody's grateful. Now piddle off and leave me, I got things to do.' Mrs Grossman wouldn't have let him talk like that.

FOUR

Mr Grossman's right. The area is a ghetto. A ghetto is a place where victims come to wait. It may spread like a cancer. It might fortify itself like a castle in a war. But all the time it waits. It never relaxes. It never sleeps. Its eyes are always open. The streets are noisy but the ghetto's voice is hushed. It waits to shout out. To scream.

A ghetto area is like a sick wolf in a hungry pack.

They're not called ghettoes; they are just boroughs of London. But that's what they are. The city is fragmenting into encampments. Society is becoming unsociable. Even the rich people live in virtual ghettoes. With their private security patrols. And their recherché cars like tanks. A different class to us. They pay someone to look over their shoulder.

In a way, every house is a ghetto. We're all in a minority group these days. We're all under pressure.

I hate this world. God must have been out of His mind. Is that blasphemy? I don't know. I don't care.

The VD clinic is like a jampot on a hot summer's day. It's busier than the latrine at Piccadilly.

From eight to eighty, everybody's there. Hookers. Midwives. Karate instructors. Priests. Babies. Did you know babies can be born with syphilis? What a bleeding great start, eh? Social workers struck by social diseases. Pest exterminators. Poets. Pensioners. Piss artists. VD viruses must be having a ball.

Get it?

It's like the Yellow Pages. Except the last I heard, only fifteen per cent of the firms in the pages are still in business. I'm not surprised. Everybody's too busy going to the VD clinic. There must be a groove in the pavement.

Jaz goes twice a week for her syphilis treatment. I go along with her, wait in the caff across the street. I don't like to go too close, in case I catch something. Even then I don't feel too safe. The way my luck runs I'll probably catch something from the caff door handle. I open it with the tip of the little finger of my left hand.

She has to queue up for nearly an hour to get her bang. They were really chafed with her because she's allergic to penicillin. They give her something called neoarsphenamine, or as Jaz calls it 'nosey-arse machine'. It's probably just something they make up round the back. I don't have a lot of faith in them.

While I wait I drink a mug of tea and surreptitiously finger the gold krugerrand which is taped to my belly button with Elastoplast.

Mr Grossman went away yesterday. Nobody knows where. He just wandered off in his night clothes and disappeared.

They'll probably find him in the river.

What a waste. He could have been a good guy if they'd let him. First thing this *matin* – he'd only been gone the night – the other tenants shared out all his gear. They shared it out in the time-honoured manner of beating the hell out of everyone and grabbing what they could. All that's left of the crippled old man is a circle of gold and an old pistol that needs a clean. Even the army blankets, full of holes and stains and thin as sacramental host, they went.

How much will I leave behind? A pile of unsatisfied grudges. A couple of enemies. A whiff of halitosis.

Another waste. Another fly speck on the dungheap of life. I'm a really cheerful guy. I go to pantomimes and glare daggers.

I should have tried chatting up the waitress in this caff, she kept looking at me. I couldn't think of anything to say. I was about to say something one time, but she turned away just as I started to speak. I felt a prick.

She kind of stopped looking when she realized I used to wait for someone from the VD clinic.

I feel sorry for waitresses. I went in one of the big department stores once, in Oxford Street. I didn't want to buy anything, I just wanted to have a look at one. I was only a kid. About twenty-two. Let's be honest, I couldn't afford to buy anything. Even a cup of tea.

The cosmetic section was on the ground floor, knee deep in scented doxies stiff with make-up. Queening over each other like professional bitches. Laughing their phoney laughs with all their white teeth. Ahuh-har-hah! That's how they laugh. With eyes like ice. Like goosed jackals. They couldn't move in case they dislodged something. I bet their bras were stuffed with talc. But they looked immaculate. Every one of them. All white.

On the top floor, in the cafeteria, the little table waitresses stood around. Clearing up people's leftovers. Wiping up the spills. And they were all coloured girls. Every one. Not a white woman in sight. Except at the tables, slurping their peegees, ahuh-har-hahing. Probably silent-farting.

Standing in the doorway, I watched one of them clearing the tables with her quick, nimble fingers; the

deft movements of the practised hand. What a waste –
to be so skilful at loading a tray.

And there were a couple of scruffy-looking bozos
sloping about, shoving trolleys and emptying bins. A
strange mixture of pretty young girls and shabby old
men. Receptionists and commissionaires. Waitresses
and kitchen helpers.

The store was full of trash anyway. I think it's closed
down now. It was probably burned out in the big
fires.

Jaz had been going to the clinic about three weeks. One
day something awful happened.

I was sitting in the caff. Bored. Watching the dregs
in my mug. It was pretty serried. There were a lot of
dildoes clamouring about.

Jaz came out the main door, stood for a moment at
the top of the steps, rapping with someone. Then she
started down, in her consuetudinary slouch. Hands in
her jacket pockets. Heels clicking. I couldn't hear
them, but they always click.

She'd changed her hair to lilac; the breeze streaked it
across her face. She shook her head. I drained my mug,
tapped it down, checked that my flies hadn't come
adrift.

From the corner of my eye, somebody strode
towards Jaz. In a white coat. Tall, striding hard, fast. I
started to turn towards him, confused for that first
moment, rising out of my seat as I swung. He was
fifteen, ten yards away from her. I looked straight at
him, right at his profile. Jaz arrived at the bottom of the
steps.

'Jasmiiine . . .!' I started to cry, hurrying to get to

121

my feet now. My chair crashed back. 'Jasmine!!' I screamed.

He slid out a gun. Stepped right up to her – she didn't know him. Bam bam! The albino blew her belly out.

Everyone was looking at me. I collided through the tables, spilling everyone out of my way. I broke the glass in the doors as I bundled out. I bombed into the middle of the street. My gun was in my fist, shaking with anticipation.

'Homer! *Homer!!*' I saw his white coat blending into the crowd. I stood there helplessly a moment. Then I heard Jasmine cry. 'Beekay? Beekay?'

She was crawling at the bottom of the steps, supporting herself on one hand. Her guts were coming out of her back.

He must have used dum dums. The holes were like screaming mouths.

'Beekay? Beekay?' Tears were flooding down her cheeks. I don't think she could see anything.

FIVE

Jaz lay in a hospital bed like an old teddy bear. She flopped in it as if she was boneless. She looked as heavy as a corpse, as though under her skin she had turned to stone. It was like Aunt Mel over again. Only worse. This time Homer had used different bullets; the girl's guts were in tatters. Belly bolognese. The great plan of the human body was spoiled beyond recognition.

She was unconscious, heedless of the entreaties of life. You couldn't wake people to that kind of torment. Her tiny eyes with their daggered lashes were stuck down fast by tapes of oblivion.

There was a tube up her nose connected to some kind of pump. And a jar at the side of the bed was slowly filling with unpleasant brown stuff. Saline was going into one arm; something else was going into the other. Lucozade maybe, I don't know. The covers were raised into a tent over her belly, like a group of fairies were camping under there. A catheter dripped patiently. Like her silent life.

There was a good chance Jaz would die. A bloody good chance. Too good, for my liking. I wanted to do something to shorten the odds, but there was nothing.

I just sat at the bedside, looking at her face. Trying to see if she was still breathing. She always was; but I was frightened. Sometimes there'd be a heartstopping pause between the frail inhalations. Sometimes she'd click in her throat.

I'd touch her hand from time to time. But there was no response, just a flush of warmth. Her grey eyes in their purple pits looked like they'd never open. They'd finished with the world. Her thin lips were cracked and split, and I kept rubbing a little of my own saliva in to moisten them.

Poor Jaz. I'd never got to know her all that well. She was a secretive girl.

Now she was really cryptic. She wasn't letting on at all. If there were any dreams going on in that little head, she wasn't about to share them with me. I sighed. I sigh a lot these days. Poor old Jaz. Seventeen years old. Sitting by the door in the waiting room of Death.

The only good thing that ever happened to her, was she won a race in junior school. She didn't even win a ma and pa. One died at the birth and the other didn't even know about it. That left a sick aunt and an uncle with a dong too hungry for him to handle. The rest is history. She started on the bottom rung and went progressively lower.

So it lies there now. A useless body that had bugger all, and had bugger all to give. What a bastard this whole scene is. It makes you want to jack it all in and become a flaming jickhead.

I've got to leave soon to get some dough. I've had to give my krugerrand as deposit. Need to go back to the Buzzard to scrape up some cash; in places like this it's cash in advance in case you die. I don't like using that money though, not while Harry's still in the can. Got no choice this time. God I'm so tired. I want to lie down in a bloody corner and die. There's fuck all goes right

for me in this life. Fuck bloody all. Even the people I
know, they all have to suffer.

I'd better make a move. I don't want them to start
pulling the frigging tubes out. God, somehow or other,
I wish it would all come to an end.

SIX

Four days fly and I'm back. Jaz is still hanging on. Just about. She looks like a glove puppet.

She put in a recovery bid for a while. But it fell through. A haemorrhage made its play. They think an infection has got into the wound, poisoned it. But she doesn't look a lot different. For someone with syphilis, bullet wounds and septicaemia she looks pretty good. I just sit around helplessly. She's the only thing I have. It's just an empty world outside this room.

I saw Mr Grossman again this morning. But he didn't notice me.

He was nailed to a warehouse door, in the crucifixion pose. He had nails through his hands and his feet. And his body was all twisted to hell where a succession of bones had dislocated. He wasn't a pretty sight.

He was still in his night clothes, a pair of grubby floral pyjamas. But they were stained dark brown with blood, stiff as neglected sails. It was hard to recognize his face. Blood had bubbled out of his nose, his mouth, had dried like tar on a scorching day; even his eyes seemed to have had a bloody weep. His countenance was like the mask of a clown struck blind in the middle of applying his make-up. All of the muscles had slumped. The cracked face was trying to slide off the skull. The dried droplets on the end of his nose seemed the worst of all. They made me want to be sick. I was sick, behind a wall.

Everyone knew who had done it. There was a crowd of about sixty, seventy, laughing about, pointing. Kids, gramps. It was a killing by Marko's squad. Their mode of internecine social amelioration. Assuming that like them you're a raving xenophobe. Or just raving.

The Pilates. The Crucifixion Squad. They used to make the front page nearly every day. Superstars.

Not having anywhere else to go, one of the nurses lets me sleep in the office when the Sister's not about. The nurse is called Sebastian.

My mother, who was a small lady, told me never to trust a big woman. My mother told me never to trust lots of things. Strange men. Strange women.

Familiar men. Familiar women. Dogs.

Jews. People with gold teeth. Protestants. Toilet seats. Foreigners. Handrails. Cracked cups.

If my paranoia could be said to have a single root, it was there. Grubbing amongst all those dreads and demons that she drummed into me while I stood gravely listening, a little kid in a tepid bathtub. My mummy. Freud would have loved her. I did, until I was about four. Then we kind of drifted apart. I think she gave me a bit of a shove off actually. I had a lot of habits she didn't like.

Momma's dead. But her fears live on. I carry them with me, in life's pouch.

Sebastian is a big woman. My mother would have hated her.

Sebastian is also probably the most beautiful girl I've ever seen. And I could fancy her like hell, except – God played a wicked prank. She's tall, almost as tall as me.

And about my age, thirty maybe. Her hair is auburn, it's feral and wilful and tumbles about her face like a storm on a mountain, like it's always autumn. Her eyes are so green you could lose an emerald. But. . . .

On the left side of Sebastian's beautiful face, from eyebrow to jawline, there is a huge purple birthmark. It looks as though the Wicked Queen cast a spell on her in the womb. Cursed her for ever with a bruise that will never heal, with the tattoo of an arcanum. It looks as though she's been kicked in the face. Which I guess she has.

And when she talks to you, she tries to hide it. That's the worst part of all. She turns her head away unconsciously. But she's so beautiful. It would make a god weep. Yet all the time, she knows it's there. And you wish you could ignore it. But you can't.

I think, if it wasn't for the naevus, I would fall in love with Sebastian Dooley. I don't know. Maybe I will anyway. God, if only she didn't have that mark. I bet that's what she says every morning.

She says she has to go to Junk City. Because of the cholera. 'Do you want to go?' I asked. What do you think? I said she should tell them to stuff it. I'm great at giving advice.

'Do you know how many qualified nurses there are out there, waiting for my job? It's like the Sword of Damocles! It's not the cholera that I'm worried about, it's the place itself. The last time they sent a team in there, it didn't come out!'

'Break a leg.'

'I wish I could!' She brushed the purple side of her face, unconsciously trying to wipe it away. She shook her head. 'You think you're so clever when you get a job. I wish I'd never bothered! I don't mind doing the work; I just don't want to get killed for it!' She had to go trotting off then because someone was screaming blue murder. Another cockroach in a bedpan probably.

I think she's worried. I don't blame her.

SEVEN

She woke me next morning with a cup of tea. Bleary-eyed, there's only one question at that hour of the day. 'What's the time?'

'Six o'clock.'

'Six o'clock!' Jesus Christ, it's the middle of the flaming night!

'Jasmine's about the same.' She lit a cigarette, turned her face away. 'I'm off now. What are you going to do?'

'I'll go get some breakfast. Sit with Jaz. Have a read.'

She nodded, left. I pulled myself together, raked through my hair in the little mirror, shambled along to the eighth bed where the ghost of Jaz lay. She looked the same; white, graven, trapped in an arcane loneliness, a million miles from help. Impenetrable. I wandered out again. Useless as a blocked drain.

There was nowhere open. Most places looked like they wouldn't be opening again. There was a lot of boarding up. A lot of falling down. It was a competition between ascendent and descendent decay. The bottom floors went first. But collapse began from the roof.

I rambled about. Little to see. Most people had decided not to join me. I can't say I blame them, the area's got nothing going for it. It exudes poverty, bitterness, tension, crime. It's the sort of area you're told to avoid when you're a kid. And then you grow up and you're living there. The sort of area churchmen remember in their prayers. And shun like the plague.

It's not even a place for the Devil. Not God, not the Devil. Right along the line, it belongs to man. He's marked it as a dog marks its territory. There are burnt-out buildings. Collapsed subways. Mausoleums of rubble. Scent marks.

Eventually I found a café opening and tried to appease my belly with a Mars Bar and a cuppa. I like a hot breakfast so I dunked the Mars in the mug. I fingered my valuables nervously. I only had one valuable – the krugerrand. I had that back again, but I didn't have any bloody money. Seventeen hundred quid they'd said; so I brought back a bit extra so I had some spare. And then they said it had gone up to twenty-five hundred because of 'restructuring and rationalization'. What the hell does that mean? It's just a rip off isn't it?

So I was back where I'd been. No place to go, no one to go with, nothing to spend when I get there. I'm like a repeat. I could have forfeited half of my life and not noticed the bloody difference.

I watched the steam slide down the paper-panelled walls. I rolled a cigarette so thin a matchstick dwarfed it. It's a bad sign when there's more paper in your fags than tobacco. It burnt like the fuse to a bomb in my mouth. I tried to swat a fly that kept landing on my lip. A dog was trying to scatch a hole in the bottom of the door.

All I could keep thinking was, as soon as Jaz gets better I'm going to put her on a boat to America, and then I'm going back for Harry. I don't care if I have to advertise for him in the bloody paper; it's time we got out of here. I should have made it happen long ago. I was beaten by my own bloody timidity.

I went back to the hospital, got a bowl of water from

131

one of the nurses, gave Jaz a wash. She seemed hotter to me. I hope that's not a bad sign. Then I read a couple of old mags, stared into space a while, cadged the odd cup of tea. And thus another day slipped through the fingers of my life. But too many of them are disappearing this way.

The day was so hot, even the bluebottles were sweating. The afternoon was suffocating. Evening came on like fire and brimstone, the sky was golden and ruddy with heat; the clouds were stretched so thin they almost drifted off into space. The western horizon was growing purpler and purpler as its high blood pressure climbed. The first bright stars had tics, and I was on the street again.

All my charm availed me nothing. I couldn't get anything to eat in the hospital. I was driven out to seek a chip shop. I followed a trail of greasy papers. My khaki jacket was heavy with sweat, but I couldn't take it off because of Mr Grossman's gun in my pocket. I didn't want that clattering on the deck and blowing my foot off.

Just to cheer me up I found I had a couple of boils coming on my neck. I told myself it could be worse; but a could be is nothing compared with what is. I was just waiting for the first symptoms of bubonic plague to appear. That's broken out in a lot of places in London recently. Typhoid, plague, we've got them all. It's like the bloody Dark Ages.

The chip shop is closed. Big surprise. I carry on, looking for someplace to eat. All the shops are hidden behind brick windows. There's no glass any more. The doors are covered with sheets of metal, and designations are painted on the walls. 'Food shop'. 'Close shop'. The 'close shop' sells clothes.

I pass an office block that's now a squatters' warren. I went in there a couple of days ago to see if there was any room. But they were hanging from the ceilings. If they haven't got typhoid already they'll have it bloody soon. The ceilings are sagging under the weight of 'elimination products'. Liquid shit is running down the walls.

I go into a little diner and get some beans on toast. It reminds me of the 'Alhambra', but worse. At least some of the whores in the Alhambra don't *look* as though they're crippled with pox. The couple in this joint look like they have to be wheeled about.

The fat guy behind the counter is so greasy they probably fry the bacon in it. He's cut his finger on the bread knife and it's dripping all over the counter. He's trying to put an old plaster about the size of a corn-pad on it. He's got an expression like a retarded chimpanzee.

I scrape up the last of the beans, have a second cup of tea. I must've fallen asleep for a little while. All of a sudden there's a lot of bangs and I'm waking up with a start. What the hell? The guy from the counter's locking all the doors and turning the lights out. One of the whores farts.

I get up and stumble to the door. The guy's struggling to slide a huge rusty bolt. 'What's going on? I don't want to be locked in here!' A lot of bangs and flashes from the street. He flings the door open. 'Gerrout then! Go on, piss off!' He shoves me out and slams the door behind me. What the hell is going on? Gordon Bennett!

It's a bloody riot!

They're spilling down the street towards me like a herd of savages! Twisted catfarts! I turn round and run! I run like a bloody madman!

133

Oh good God, they're in front of me too! A huge mass is billowing round a corner like a cloud of hooligans. Jesus Christ! I panic. My heart plays allegro. Mother*rr*!!

It floods around me. Everything is swimming for its life, the street is bucking up and down. I pick myself up, dusting the grit out of my scuffed hands. Oof! bodies slamming into me, spinning me about. Houses wheel and teeter.

I rush along with the mob. The police are right behind. Then they're in front! They're coming from all directions! So is the mob. It's a bloody free-for-all! Jesus Christ! A gun goes off right by my ear and nearly blows my brains out of my nose. A woman dashes into me and the top of her head bashes my nose. It's coming in for a lot of stick. I stagger back dazed, waiting for the blood to start blooping out, but nothing comes. I shake my head. I look round for a way to go.

What should I do? The hospital – I've got to get back to the hospital. Which way's that? Gordon Bennett, they're throwing fucking bricks at me now! I cower in a doorway and cradle my head. Waugh! one of them belts me in the ribs!

I scramble up, dash along a wall, pushing people out of the way, one arm crooked defensively in front of my mush. Gorblimey, there are kids and everything here! I've just fallen over a bloody pushchair. There's nobody in it.

Which way is the flaming hospital? Must be down there. Ow! Something hits me on the side of the face. I lean against a wall, gasping and cursing, cradling my cheek. There's a stain of blood across my hand when I look at it. And I'm still being buffeted and shoved, no time to draw a bloody breath even. In a sudden fit of temper I turn around and kick out at someone, viciously. But they're pissed to the gills and don't even notice. Hurts my bloody toe through, should've remembered I've only got plimmies on.

Tutting and muttering I struggle across the street, knocked down a couple of times by flying louts. There must be about eleven thousand people crammed into a postage stamp fragment of the *A to Z*, and most of them are running into me.

And specks of gunfire, like the squall before the storm, speak out above the din, indignant. 'Oi!' That's what the guns say. 'Oi! You!' And somebody falls, or just stumbles, or is carried away. Or just lies there. What's all that bloody smoke?

I go about fifty yards down the street to the turning to the hospital, dodging the missiles and bodies that are whizzing about like it's Guy Fawkes Night. What a din! You've never heard so much noise! Screaming, yelling, whooping. Breaking glass. Bottles, cans, tear gas, shotguns. Buildings are on fire. I zip around the corner, crouching low in the hope they won't shoot kids. The goddamn hospital is on fire!

Shit almighty! Smoke is gushing out of the place. There are red patients dancing terrified at the windows. But they're not patients, they're flames! Holy Mother, Jasmine's in there! I pelt across the road, running hard like a schoolkid in a race. Get out of the bloody way you bastards, get out of the way!

A line of dingoes is trying to shepherd folk from the place. The first two storeys are really vomiting in the flames, great gouts of whitish smoke are heaving out. There's an excruciating cacophony of glass and screaming.

I push my way to the front of the crowd – an erratic line of serge backs ahead of me. Beyond that the hospital concourse, the main entrance thronged with comers and goers, helpers and victims. Bandages all over the place, shrieking and yelling like birds on a tip.

No sign of any fire appliances. Even if they're roadworthy they can't get through. And there are other buildings on fire; a dozen, twenty of them, tenement blocks, the police station.

I batter my way on, through the police line, stumbling over their stupid feet. Smoke tumbling down into our faces. I make it up the steps, nearly crushed by a bloody bedside cabinet that someone flings out of an upstairs window.

I shove a few buggers out of the way, claw and wriggle inside, go back to pick up an old crone that I've just knocked for six. She clings to my arm, winded. I shove her glasses back into place, push her towards the street. I struggle back in.

The place is alive with mayhem. It's coming out of the walls. The stairs are choked, deafened with people trying to get down. A tide of human misery – who said that? Anyway it's here. I dive into them. I've got to get to the third floor. You can hear things cracking and exploding in the flames.

What a bloody game. I'm being knocked back as fast as I can climb up. People pushing me in the face and falling on to me. I climb over the handrail, crush my goddamn nuts, struggle up the narrow outer step, clinging on like grim death. I think my hands are sweating – they are, but most of it is blood and slime from the rail. You've never seen so much mess. People are leaking in all directions.

It's like a mass of cattle fleeing the slaughterhouse. I

make it to the landing, climb back over. Just about. Some bright spark struggling with a stretcher backs into me just as I'm at my most precarious moment. I grab him round the throat to save myself. He drops the stretcher. The woman in it rolls off with a great groan. Sorry love, I haven't the time to be polite. I bomb down the corridor into the ward. It's nearly empty. Jasmine's still there, oblivious to it all.

What the hell am I going to do – she's connected to all these tubes and things. Where's Sebastian? She comes out of a side ward, her uniform's grey with sweat. 'Seb! Seb!'

She hurries over. 'What about Jasmine?' She looks around the ward, sweat dripping off her nose. Just a couple of old people left, asleep or unconscious. They're probably dead anyway. She bites her lip. A huge bore of thick black smoke comes tumbling up the stairs and a terrible screaming breaks out below. 'We'll take her down the fire escape!' The old people will have to take their chance. Maybe someone will save them.

The fire escape is crowded. My vertigo hits me for a minute and I waver. I'm looking out over smoking rooftops. The evening has darkened suddenly to a deep navy, the buildings are poised shadows, like hungry dogs.

Jasmine's heavy in my arms, limp as bolts of cloth. I pick a space and step out on to the metal platform – three storeys above us, three below. Seb squeezes right behind, holding the tubes out of harm's way. But you can bet your life it's got its bloody eye on them.

There are enormous booms from one of the neighbouring streets. A terrific crash as a roof subsides. We inch down, a step at a time. The flights are steep, guaranteed to send you hurtling. More and more people bundle out on to them. Blankets and sheets go sailing past. My arm muscles start to throb. It's the slowness that does it.

All of a sudden the flaming thing pulls out of the wall with an almighty lurch. I crash into the rails, teeter hideously for a moment with my clumsy burden, thirty feet above the ground – all the night swoons before me, my guts disappear into my trouser legs.

There's a crack like gunfire, the upper staircase breaks away at a seam, goes shrieking to the ground. Right on the brink of the crack, Sebastian topples back, grabs at my hair for support. Her legs slide away, she crashes to her knees, splitting them to the bone on the torn edge, where the rusty rivets gave way. She screams. I scream – she's ripping my bleeding scalp off!

I'm bent over backwards like a bloody limbo dancer. I start to give. She grabs my trouser leg, hauls herself back on, just before my spine snaps, releases her grip. But the blood bottle has burst, all the tubes have ripped out of Jasmine's arms. I stand for a moment agonized. Then the fire escape gives another little shudder, and we bugger off down the stairs as fast as we can go. About ten feet from the bottom I lose my footing, crash down on my spine. The bump nearly rams my backbone out of the top of my head. My brain swims.

By the time we make the ground we're a pair of goddamn cripples. We stagger along the wall crying. I'm nearly blinded by the pain in my head, and there's so much blood on Sebastian's legs it looks like the skin has been scoured off. Jaz sleeps through it all. There are sixty, eighty people, lying in the tangled ribcage of the broken staircase. We ignore them.

EIGHT

The goddamn street is trying to tear us to bits. Dense crowds all about. Madmen to the left of us, madmen to the right. Out of the hospital concourse poured the sick wounded. Jesus Christ, the air is humming with bricks and bottles! We struggle on hunched over, both of us trying to shield Jasmine. Her head is lolling carelessly.

We're surrounded by police. And the mob wants their guts. They're flinging themselves at them like wolves. Smoke is just dumped on us until everyone is running round streaming tears. And the noise goes on, and on and on. Howling, baying, roaring for blood.

And it doesn't matter whose. People on rooftops are slinging down slates like guillotines. There are bodies lying all over the place, bleeding, groaning, spewing out slime. There are more broken faces than at the scene of an explosion in a clock factory. The incessant, remorseless, maddening din makes your head want to burst. It makes you just want to screw up your eyes and pound your head to a pulp. Will you shut up? For Christ's sake, will you shut that noise and just let me think! They're driving me out of my bloody mind!

Suddenly we're being bundled into a hall or something. A school hall, church hall, I don't know. I'm falling over the bloody steps. There's about forty coppers, me and Seb, half a dozen other patients. We've all got blood on us, like badges. What's going on, what's going on?

A fusillade of missiles follows us, raining down like a tarmacadam cloudburst. Fucking hell! Bouncing off our goddamn heads! We scurry inside, slam the doors behind us. The crowd flings itself against them.

A sergeant screams. 'Get them benches! Get them benches!' They grab half a dozen wooden benches, try to jam the doors with them. It's useless. You might as well say abracadabra. The doors lurch inwards, just about to puke. The sergeant pulls out his pistol. Blam blam blam! He empties the clip through the doors. There's a lot of screaming. The crowd drops back. They bolt the doors again. Pile up a barricade. 'Watch the windows! Watch the bloody windows!' We cower in a corner, wailing.

We're trapped in this goddamn hall. I'm a wanted man, a desperate criminal, and I'm locked in a room full of furies. How the hell do I get into these situations? Why does it always happen to me?

After two hours the noise outside has scarcely diminished. It must be a machine, everyone should be hoarse by now. We crouch in the darkness. The lights have gone, sole illumination is the flame light flooding erratically through the small windows. Most of the windows are broken. No they're not, they're all broken.

We line a few bunks along one wall – they were unearthed in a dusty cupboard in the other room. There's a toilet, but it's blocked and beginning to leak under the door. The blueboys stand around in little clusters, listening to their radios, occasionally gabbling to them.

We lay the patients on the beds. I heap jackets up on

top of Jaz. Even in the gloom I can see that her colour is awful. Her face looks olive. What's that – jaundice? I daren't ask Seb, she's struggling to stop some old guy busting open all his stitches as he heaves his stomach all over the floor. She's crying because of the pain in her legs. With the naevus black in the eldritch light, it looks like she's wearing a mask.

I squat on the floor like a useless prick. What if one of the coppers recognizes me? What if the crowd outside sets fire to the goddamn place? It's brick, they won't do that. They seem to have forgotten us for the moment. The sergeant says they're dropping tear gas on them from helicopters. You can sniff it in here.

Spirits in my boots. What the hell's going to happen next? What is it about me? I must have been born under a bad star. I search through my pockets for a fag. Nothing. Dropped 'em. Oh sodding hell. I think I'm doomed to a life of bad luck. If I live to be thirty it'll be a miracle. If I live to be twenty-nine it'll be a goddamn miracle – and that's the day after tomorrow!

A great roar goes up from the crowd. Somebody's scored a goal. I climb on a chair, peek from a window. Another building on fire. The squatters' den, the old office block. Look at them, leaping out of the window like mice. I suppose there's always someone worse off than yourself.

I climb down. I check on Jaz. She's as still as a church. I adjust the jackets, find a terrible cold patch on her belly. Cold and wet. I pull my hand away – sticky blood. At the same moment the hall comes under attack again, a bunch of crazy youths. Got to find Sebastian.

Wow! I squeak as something sails through a window and whizzes past my head. A lump of tarmac shaped like Australia. It bounces off somebody's face, pushes

141

most of their nose into their skull. That's the trouble with being blind, you can't see them coming. Poor bugger. Still, it gives him something to think about.

I scrabble across the floor, under the line of beds. Eight beds. I bang my head eight times. I'm nearly bloody senseless by the time I reach the end. I look around stupidly.

God, it's noisy as hell in here. It sounds like Pandora's just opened her bean can. I feel like a character in a Doré painting. I croak, 'Sebastian? Sebastian!' Where the hell is she? 'Sebastian, for Christ's sake!' I can't see a damn thing. Well, I can, but nothing recognizable.

I scuttle into the other room. Pick up a splinter from the wooden floor. 'Sebastian?'

'Who's that?'

'It's me. Beekay.'

'Who?'

'Beekay.'

'Come here son, will you?' It's an old woman. Another of life's strangers. Another piece of flotsam washed up on the beach of my experience. She looks about a hundred and eighty, wrapped in a blanket on the floor. She presses something into my hand. A tiny gold watch. 'Give that to my daughter will you? If anything happens to me.'

'I don't know your daughter.'

'That's a good boy.' She squeezes my hands.

Complete impotence numbs me. Life's bad enough without having pitiful people thrusting themselves on you. Bastards I can cope with; this kind of thing screws me up. 'You're not going to die love,' I say. I squeeze her shoulders. As much for my comfort as hers.

'Don't let *them* get it!' she jerks her head. 'Them blacks!'

'They're not all blacks.' What's the point though? Nobody wants their prejudices correcting. Least of all old people. I sit there for a minute, my arm around her shoulders. Why didn't she give it to the goddamn police? Maybe she thinks they're worse than the blacks. She's trembling. She must have caught it from me.

More explosions in the street make it difficult for me to sit there with her. I feel too vulnerable. I put the watch in her lap, sneak away. I can hear her coughing into her hanky, with a cough like a sparrow's. I hope she doesn't have to sneeze, she'll kill herself.

God, I wish I was somewhere else. A voice penetrates the din. 'Hello Beak.'

'Where've you been? I've been looking all over for you.' I grab her hand.

'Has something happened?'

'Yeah. I think she's bleeding again.'

We scurry back and Seb goes to work in that strangely detached way that nurses have. I don't take my eyes off her. It helps to keep the noise at bay. And the *Angst*. Oh God, don't let her die, Seb.

I wonder what it's like to die? Do your thoughts gradually fade away, fighting against extinction with desperate, terrified futility? Or do you just go, snuff! Like that? I wonder if you're dead before you even know it?

Sebastian works on Jasmine silently for some minutes. There's not a lot she can do, this fusty old hall is hardly equipped for medical emergency. I'm filled with an awful chill, crouching in the darkness. Come on Seb, you can do it.

She licks her lips. She looks around the dusky room as if seeking help. Blood is oozing through the pad pressed

143

on Jaz's stomach. The detached calm of the nurse is dissolving rapidly.

'How's she doing Seb?' I know how she's doing. I can see with my own scared eyes that she's dying. But I have to say something. God, what happened to all the goddamn doctors?

Seb looks at me, she's upset too. 'I can't do anything, Beak. I can't do anything.'

I look at her for a minute, desperation growing. 'Maybe I could go and find a doctor!'

Seb shakes her head sadly. 'She'd probably die anyway, Beak.'

Jasmine must have heard her. She gives a sudden cough, coughs up blood. Seb tries to hold her still. She begins convulsing, sounds in her throat like she's about to vomit. Shudders kick through her. I hold her down. Both of us trying to hold her still, to stop this frantic pushing. Every muscle gives a tremor. Jasmine's face contracts, for a moment she almost wakes. Then a terrible, deep cry emerges from her throat. She subsides. A dreadful stillness settles on her. Then out of the blue, another dry groan.

I stare at her dementedly. Determined that she's still alive. Crazy, for a moment. But Seb prises my fingers from the thin arms. 'She's dead Beak.'

I just stared ahead numbly. Dead. Dead because she knew me. It's not fair. It isn't goddamn fair! Tears spill out of me.

NINE

Morning comes, cloying, smelling, crawling with flies. Another bitter morning, angry with the state of men. Angry with me. Hating me.

I rub my knuckles in my eyes. God, the smell in here is bad. You could butter your bread with the air. It drags itself in through the broken windows like a tired old man.

I sit dully, letting other folk do all the moving about. Outside it's quiet. But it's not over. It's the pause between rounds, when wounds are licked and hatred stews. We couldn't leave the hall. I have nowhere to go anyway. Maybe downhill a bit further, that's about all.

A few feet away Jaz's body lies in a bundle, wrapped in an old red curtain. Tied at the head and feet with a couple of wire coathangers I found in one of the cupboards. She looks like something put out for a jumble sale.

Flies are crawling all over the cloth. It doesn't take them long to get the smell. In this heat, it doesn't take anyone long.

Seb is dozing, flaked out on a cot. She looks like a battered wife or something, arms akimbo, the side of her face purple like a bruise. I wonder if she'll ever get married, with that birthmark? She's snoring gently as if she's shy about it. I fumble through my pockets again. Still no bloody smokes. This is no time to have to give up. I'd ask one of the *carabinieri* but I need to keep a low profile.

That's about the only thing going for me. I'm so insignificant nobody notices me. God, I'm so tired. My eyes are like a marathon runner's blisters. All that tear gas. All that staying awake.

'Ciggy?' I look up. It's the sergeant. A bumpkin of a man, with cheeks like rosy red areolae. Spiky grey hair sticking up like filings on a magnet. He's got a bogie caught just inside his nose.

'Thanks.' He strikes a match against the wall. But it's gloss paint and won't ignite. In the end I light the things with my sputtering lighter, courtesy of Woolworths. One day I must go back and pay for it.

'Been a long night.'

Oh God, he's a bloody chit-chatter. 'Aye.'

'Got caught up in it did you?'

No, I came looking for it, what do you think? 'Aye.'

'Bloody animals. I'd shoot the bloody lot of them.' He jerked his head at Sebastian. 'Is she your girlfriend?' I shook mine. 'Shame about that mark innit? She'd be all right, 'cept for that. Good tits.'

I snorted inwardly. You pathetic, predictable little man. I hope he gets clubbed to death with his own truncheon. I've got no time for pillocks.

He yawned, glanced at his watch, shook it. His radio crackled unintelligibly. He put his hand in his trousers, adjusted himself. Wiped his hand on his leg. 'Hot, innit?'

I nodded. 'It's this bloody heat does it.'

He laughed. 'Aye.' One of life's natural comedians aren't I? 'I always get a sort o' rash, just 'ere in the crack o' me bum. D'you get that?' I looked away. These people seem to home in on you like wasps. He sniffed an

146

armpit. 'Be glad to get out o' this lo'. Smells like a fuckin' tart's old knickers.'

'How long do you think we'll be here?'

'Ah, not long, not long now. They've got the bloody army coming in at nine o'clock. That'll clear the bastards.'

'How's that? I thought the army weren't supposed to interfere.'

He shrugged. 'It's all the fuckin' same innit? As long as they get their bleedin' 'eads split open, dun matter who does it, does it?' He sighed. 'Nah, they wanna get the bloody flame-throwers on 'em,' he said vehemently. 'They wanna sterilize the bastards!'

I stubbed out my fag without much vehemence. The hunger in my stomach was just about dissecting me. It went from just below my ribs, through the small of my back, to my bum. Even my eyeballs were peckish. I'm always hungry. My metabolism's going all to hell.

Sebastian stirred on the cot; the sergeant moved away; I tried again to get a splinter out of a finger. 'What time is it?' she asked. I shrugged. 'Did you get any sleep?'

I shook my head. 'Too much noise. I think I dozed off once or twice.' The trouble with dozing off is that you can never be sure you've actually done it. She looked wiped out. Her skin was blotchy, her good looks hadn't had a chance to get themselves together. She looked a bit bemused. She looked chilly. It must be shock or something, it's not cold in here. I took her hands, gave them a rub to warm them. 'What's happening outside?'

I shrugged again. God, if other people were as rude as me. . . .

I'm too goddamned tired to care. Even for Sebastian, I'm just too weary. I look around. The lawmen are

147

looking like lawmen again. Tugging on their rounded boots, buckling their belts. Fiddling with their collars and crutches. Belching, stretching, all the usual manly things. Sebastian struggles up, biting her lip as her legs protest. The wounds still won't heal. She goes to check on the patients. They've had a quiet night – too damn scared to make a peep.

The hall looks grey in the dusty early light. I look at my hands; they look grey too. I don't think I've got enough blood in my body. I flex my eyelids. Jesus Christ, my eyes are raw. I seem to have a permanent tic in the left one; it's driving me round the bloody twist.

Sebastian limps back. She must be in agony, her face is full of pain. 'How is everybody?' I ask.

'That old woman in the other room's gone. I think she died of fright.'

She knew she was going to die. That's always a bad sign. 'Did she have a watch on?'

Sebastian shrugs. 'I didn't see one.' It figures. But I can't help another sigh. The brainless ones gather round the sergeant, getting their instructions hammered into them. 'Have you got any ciggies?' I shake my head. 'You don't like those coppers do you?'

'Me?' I shrugged. 'I can live without them.'

'You frightened they'll recognize you?'

A sudden chill. 'Me? How do you mean?'

'You look guilty all the time! And I've seen that gun in your pocket.'

'It's a cigarette lighter.'

'What do you smoke – dum-dums?'

Ha ha. I would have laughed but just at that moment someone fired a flaming shotgun through one of the windows. I threw Seb to the floor. Four of the dingoes went down yelling, holding their legs and faces. The coppers emptied their guns wildly. It had started again.

I suddenly realised just how much I must like Sebastian. I was lying on top of her to shield her. Or maybe we just landed that way.

Pretty soon there was a pitched battle in the street. In fact all the streets of the neighbourhood.

And we were suffering. We were in chaos. The last couple of minutes had been anarchic. Some buggers had picked up a couple of tear-gas canisters and lobbed them through the windows. We had to get out.

We were nearly having a riot of our own; bozos bombing about like mad things. They started ripping away the barricade. I ran to Sebastian and grabbed her hand. 'We'd better stick together!' I yelled. She nodded. Her arm was crooked around her face to shield it.

The doors burst open. Just got a glimpse of absolute bedlam outside, like some crazy puppet theatre gone wrong. The police charged out yelling and blasting off. I picked Jasmine's body up – I wasn't going to leave it here for those bastards to kick around. There was an awful smell as I lifted her. Her viscera slopped and gurgled, bumping about in her belly. She wasn't Jasmine any more.

We stumbled out. We had to leave the patients behind. Sometimes you've just got to look to yourself. The seething mob closed around us. We bowled down the street, caught up in a stunning clamour. Bloody mayhem. There was no way out.

After about fifty yards we got separated. I turned round to try to find her, was knocked off my pegs. There was a ghastly moment when all I could see was legs and boots stamping all about me, and I struggled madly to get up before I drowned. But I let go of Jasmine, and before I could recover I was shoved twenty yards away. There was no way I could get back. I just had a glimpse of people trampling over her and the curtain pulling apart. Then she was lost, and I was swept on. No sign at all of Sebastian. I was on my own again.

I struggled to get to the side of the road, took shelter in a doorway. The street was full of smoke. Somewhere nerve gas had been used – bozos running past were ripping at their twisted faces with their fingernails. They'd kill themselves by the time they finished. My own lungs were smarting. I leant against the door, cradling my face in my arms. All the strength had been buffeted out of my limbs. I could have stood it if I hadn't been on my own. Everything was going wrong again. My legs were quivering.

Then someone pressed something cold and circular into the back of my neck. 'All right Howard – put your hands over your head. Don't try any fancy stuff!' Just what I needed, I'm going to be arrested now! I groaned.

'David, I just nearly shat myself!'

He was grinning like a moron.

'You're a bloody pillock!'

'It was good though, wasn't it?'

'Good! I nearly had a heart attack! What are you doing here anyway, I thought you were dead!'

'Nah.' He slid a couple of bent puffers from his breast pocket, calm as ever in the midst of all this calamity. 'I would have been, if those bloody Irish had had anything to do with it. They're bloody crackers you know! They only wanted to take on the whole bloody army camp, just because we happened to have the armoury open!'

'So what happened?'

'I buggered off. I was trying to follow you, but I got shot going over the bridge.'

'What bridge?'

'The one over the river.'

'We didn't go over the bridge, we went through the woods.'

'Oh. That's probably why I lost you then.'

'Where did they shoot you?' I was looking round him for bulletholes. 'Is it bad?'

'No, it was just in the shoulder. I mean it hurt, but it wasn't the sort of thing to kill you.' He waggled his arm up and down, rubbed it. 'It's stiff, you know. Anyway, I went to my sister's in Ilford. I've been staying there the last few weeks.'

'But how did you know I was here?'

'You were on the telly. When you were coming out of the hospital, on the fire escape, they had a camera on you.' He gestured with his eyes. 'There are cameras all over the place. Who was that with you, was it Jasmine?'

I sighed out a lungful of smoke. Nodded. I took a deep breath, got it over with. 'She's dead, Dave. Homer shot her – then all this fucking lot. She died in the night.'

'Oh Christ.' He turned away with a huge sigh. He stared up for a while at the still blazing hospital, sighed again. 'Homer again. Shit.' He liked Jaz a lot.

He smoked his cigarette to its end. 'So it's just the two of us then.'

'Yeah. Maybe even less than that. I thought, maybe I'd try to get him.' There's nothing to lose now, the bastard's going to get me anyway, wherever I am. America will have to wait. This thing at least has to be done. You can't turn your back on it for ever. Not even me; even I can't do that.

David nodded. 'I guess it's time. Do you think we can?'

That's a daft question to ask an optimist like me. 'No. Do you?'

He shrugged, changed the subject. 'We've got to get out of here.'

'The army's coming in.'

'Yes, I know. That's why I came down to find you. It's going to be a bloody massacre.' He handed me a pistol and a couple of clips. 'You'd better take these. You might need them.'

'I've got one. I'm not much cop at shooting people anyway.'

'You can always throw it at them. My sister's boyfriend is a Special Con in the CDs . . .' the Civil Disturbance Section, '. . . he says they're going to kill as many as they can. They're going to try to end the riots with a show of strength. They figure this'll be the one to do it. Narrow streets, nowhere to run.'

'They can't do that.'

He shrugged. He nodded at the figures running past. 'All these guys are headed for the waste ground. That's where the police are concentrated. They think it's a bloody game. Soon as they're all up there – the army's going to come in from behind.'

'But most of these people are just –'

'What the hell do they care about that? Anyway, it's not our worry. Come on, we'd better make a move, or we'll end up in the middle of it.' He stepped out of the doorway, stopped. 'Fucking hell. They're here already!'

I peered past him. Two army trucks had pulled across the bottom of the street. Soldiers clattered out. They didn't even stop to check the wind; they just opened fire. Jesus Christ! David took off. I went with him, sticking to his heels like a nervous bride.

Across the street. We climbed a concrete wall, jumped to the ground. My ankles didn't break. David punched a drunk who tried to embrace us, smashed him in the nose with his gun.

We stretched into a run, a loping stride. We stuck close to a long wall, trying to keep low. A dingo took aim at us. David shot him in the face, blew the guts of his brain out of the back of his head. I winced, moved a bit closer. We jumped a couple of bodies. The noise was godawful.

People were stumbling all over the place, trying to get out. Trapped between the police and the army. They were demented. So was I, I was yelling like an idiot.

David nipped round a corner just ahead of me, suddenly darted back like he'd been goosed. He crashed into me, knocked me to the ground. I heard his gun go off half a dozen times. He dragged me up, pulled me on. Three soldiers were lying on the ground, clutching body wounds. They wouldn't be swigging ale for a while. He kicked a gun away from one of them. 'Give me your gun.' We swapped pistols. I reloaded for him. We were really neck-breaking it.

We stop for a moment to get our bearings. A chattering from above. Someone in a chopper has opened up with a machine gun, spraying bullets into the crowd. What the hell is this? This was just a bloody riot – they're hunting them down like dogs! I guess the war does this to people. But who the hell authorizes this kind of thing? David empties his clip at the hovering machine. But it's a waste of time. He gives up, sprints off. I'm with you buddy.

But my lungs are gasping. My face is drawn so tight it's become cement. I can't unclench my teeth. The machine in my chest is going nineteen to the dozen. Maybe twenty.

We dart into an open doorway. We scoot through an abandoned house, out the back. Clamber over a wall. Some poor bazonka's having a crap in the alley, face like terror. We gallop past, dash into a quieter street. Should be safe now. Ough – Jesus! I tumble like a heap of rubbish. A ricochet has hit me in the stomach. A plastic bullet. Oh Jesus, Jesus! A shapeless badge of blood wells through my shirt.

I'm on my knees, feeling pains shoot down into my thighs, into my shoulders. There's a great furrow across my belly. Blood bubbles out. I grind my eyes to crush out the tears. The gun clatters on the ground.

David grabs my juddering face. 'Are you okay, Beak? Are you okay?' What a bleeding stupid question. I can't speak. I just drip. My muscles have locked so tight I can barely breathe.

He lifts me up. Hell's teeth – the pain goes right through me. It's like I've got a chainsaw in my guts. Christ, why do people have to do this kind of thing to you? My legs give. I slump against him.

Oh Jesus, is this how my mother's only son is to end? Dripping to death for a lump of twisted plastic? I want to cough but daren't. I can hardly move my legs, the thighs have gone strangely numb. But David drags me on, his shoulder tucked beneath me.

I take a squinty look back. A spoor of blood is dogging us, weaving about like a sot. I must have lost eight gallons of the stuff, it's everywhere. My jeans are sodden with it. I'm drenched with sweat. It's coming out of my ears. My nose is dripping. I think I'm going to faint.

TEN

But I didn't die or anything dramatic like that. I didn't even faint more than about fifteen times. I just groaned a lot and sobbed and oozed nitid gobs of blood on to the streets of London.

David took me to an hombre he knows. A vet. Which is when most of the fainting occurred. The guy's also a tosspot. He took the lump of pink plastic out, put eleven black stitches in. He gave me the bullet as a souvenir but I lost it. That's the trouble with having open-plan pockets.

He said watch out for blood poisoning. Which is not the sort of thing to say to a bloke like me. I'd be up in the middle of the night, examining the wound by torchlight. Wondering what the hell blood poisoning looks like. Does your blood turn green or what?

But nothing happened. After a couple of weeks I got drunk and took the stitches out. And I just have a livid and very ugly line, like a radioactive centipede traversing my navel. That's twice I've been shot. It's threatening to become a trend.

So, that was that then. Another insanely hectic interlude. And two more people had been snatched away from me. My life seems to proceed in bursts, acute boredom punctuated by periods of precipitous terror. I'm either disregarded completely or I'm in the firing line.

You're lucky I don't tell you the boring bits. You'd

yawn so much your jaw would lock. Anyway, just to fill you in on the details, we're staying at David's sister's, while she's away for a couple of weeks, visiting their mum.

It's probably as well she's not here. I've been crippled with terrible wind ever since my accident. Must have shaken me up inside. Every time I walk across the room I leave a trail of minor explosions. I can't help it.

We've really got to get down to figuring out the next move. Got to get to Homer before the anger wears off. That's how he always keeps ahead of us; he's always filled with hatred. Life's slipping by too fast to waste much more of it; we're getting old. And my conscience is really starting to nag me about Harry and Rachel.

You know, all things considered, I'm a lucky kind of
guy. I get good luck, bad luck. Most of it stinks. But at
least I get it. Fate doesn't ignore me.

I was pretty lucky about that gun that Mr Grossman
gave me.

Today, being September the something, we took the
krugerrand to a little jeweller's in Hatton Garden. We
needed some dough. Don't we always? We wanted to
get some gear before we made our next uneasy play.
What day is it today? Tuesday, Wednesday, something
like that. The area's pretty quiet. Nice sunny day like
this, everyone will be down at the beach. (That's a little
joke.) A few people are combing the gutters, the alleys,
looking in the dustbins. If anything's thrown away,
someone will find a use for it.

Me and my chum David kick our heels. There's no
rush. We're not looking forward to tomorrow. Like if
we were going to a wedding, there'd be shotguns in all
directions. We're going into Junk City. The very name
gives me the willies.

I limp along with one foot in the gutter. My famous
kid's walk. My co-pain kicks a cigarette pack. My
stomach's a deal better, but the boils at the back of my
neck are pretty painful. They're supposed to be caused
by something in the blood. Maybe I have got blood
poisoning after all? I need something to worry about.

A bell in a church somewhere chimes nine times.

Which is odd, as it's eleven o'clock, but you can't have everything. I break an Aero in half and we share it. I'm a bit off Mars Bars.

We talk about the latest unemployment figures. Seventy-two per cent. We debate what's likely to happen when it reaches almost a hundred. I reckon there won't be much difference. They'll probably just stage another major battle in Europe. David says we'll all die. He's a happy soul isn't he? I'm a bloody optimist compared with some people.

We reach Hatton Garden. Most of the area's boarded up. The building opposite is falling down. It looks as though the occupants have taken to diving through the walls. We wander along for thirty minutes or so, sizing up the scene. A few dingoes about, but they don't pay us much mind. They're too busy flipping coins at walls. The old games are still the best.

We settle on a joint. David meanders off to wait in a doorway; best not to put all your eggs in the spin-dryer. I go inside. A bell tinkles. Coo-ee! It's only a tiny place, like a lavatory with gems. But not many. It's mostly watches, watching me blankly, clicking their tongues.

Classy dive though. It's got carpet on the floor. These days if it's got a door that doesn't fall off I'm pretty impressed. The lights are flickering like they are about to die. You get used to it. We spend half our lives sitting in the dark. The power only comes on long enough for them to find something else to go wrong. I think the government's behind it.

From the gloom at the rear a figure scuttles forward. It could be Mr Grossman's brother. There is also a woman. Who could be his daughter, or she could be stuffed. She doesn't move. Not a bloody flicker. I give her a little nod and a smile, but they splinter against her walls. You need therapy baby.

The man arches his eyebrows, a nervous twitch or he's saying hello. I put my coin down. It clatters on the scratched glass surface. It lies there like the eye of a dragon. 'I'd like to sell that.' I sneeze. It must be all the guy's dandruff getting up my nose.

The old man looks at it suspiciously. Probably wondering if he can melt the coin down before the real owner turns up. He picks it up between a thumb and finger. Always a good way to pick something up.

'A krugerrand, eh? A krugerrand. Haven't seen one of them for a long time.' He holds it up for the green-dressed, dark-haired dame to see. 'A krugerrand!' The woman, who must be about my age, blinks, with the look of a doll. She must be on something. Probably the lights are getting to her. They're driving me round the flaming bend.

He weighs it in his palm. He looks impressed, nods at me. 'Heavy.'

I nod back. 'I gave up making the paper ones.'

A gargle in his throat. Could have been a chortle or derision. I change feet. I must be getting old, I can't slouch for as long as I used. He takes a step towards a door at the back. 'I'll just get my stuff. Have to test it, you know.' I nod.

I look over the watches while he's gone. 'Do you want to buy a watch?' She blurts it out like a hiccup. She inclines towards me but her feet don't move. Probably the owner nails her down so she doesn't wear the carpet out.

'How much is the cheapest?'

'Hundred and twenty.'

'A hundred and twenty! Hell's teeth!' I couldn't

160

afford to ask her the time at that price. That krugerrand must be worth millions.

'We've got some broken ones for fifteen.'

'Do they work?'

'Sometimes they do.'

Thanks a bunch. I look over some wedding rings. 'Do you sell many of these?' She shrugs. This is a great conversation. The old man comes back, hunches over the gold, starts tinkering about.

A couple of minutes amble through my life. But only those watches notice. The chick stares at me. Every movement of mine acuminates her distrust. She doesn't like the way I look at things. She doesn't like the way I breathe. It's okay sister, you don't drive me crazy either.

The gem-peddler's head pops above his shoulders. He's like a bird. He does everything but twitter. He'll probably do that in a minute. He taps my dragon's eye on the glass. 'It's good.' That's one worry out of the way then.

'Do you want to buy it?'

'How much do you want?'

'How much is it worth?'

He looks doubtful. 'I could give you – a hundred.'

'A hundred!' Pull the other one cock! I've been looking at jewellers' trays all morning! 'I could sell you a bag of chocolate money for more than that!' I mean, I don't mind being ripped off; but I don't want to be torn to shreds.

He shuffled his wings. 'What do you say then?'

'A grand.' Well, at least something makes him laugh.

Just then the door nearly flings itself off its hinges. As I turn around I catch a glimpse of the peddler pedalling for the back door. I look back at him, but he's already vanished. I'm not surprised, the guys who've just come in don't look like Jehovah's Witnesses.

Trouble is, it's not him they're after! They come up to me. Uh-oh. Please God, let them be Jehovah's Witnesses. One of them picks up my krugerrand. 'Is this yours?'

I'd like to say 'What's it got to do with you mush?' But they're huge. They're so big their mothers must have had extension wombs built. Anyway they flash a badge. Oh dear, Lily Law. No wonder the guy went out the back. He's seen trouble like this before.

There was always a chance this would happen. It's all to do with profit margins. It's because not only will he get a reward for reporting me, he'll probably be in for a cut of the krugerrand when it accidentally disappears at the end of proceedings. It's murder when they start twisting honesty like this, you don't know whether it's best just to rob them, or take a chance.

'Are you deaf?'

'Er, yes, it's mine.' God, I'm for it now.

'Where'd you get it?'

'A guy gave it to me. Mr Grossman. We used to share the same building.'

'He can verify that can he?'

I nearly said, 'Of course he can't, he's dead.' But I caught myself in time. 'Sure,' I squeak.

'Sure he can.' They were both itching to thump me. 'You got your ID?'

'Er –'

'You'd better come down the nick with us.'

I started to tremble. 'I haven't done anything.'

'Put your hands on the counter.'

'But I haven't done anything. It's mine.' I can feel my bottom lip going into its familiar bounce.

It's not wise to hesitate. Bloody stupid in fact. Before I can remember that I'm winging across the room into the wall. Oof! God, my scar nearly burst open. I hang there dazed, waiting for my senses to catch me up. My legs get kicked apart as if I'm some mare at stud. They go through my pockets. Mr Grossman's gun surrenders into their hands without a fight. It's not my day. I would have been better off holding up the place. Sometimes it just doesn't pay to be honest.

We leave in a bunch. My arm is gripped in a mountainous fist that looks like it could take on my whole body with one finger tied behind its back. And still win. It's covered in sucked warts and scabby knuckles. It's horrible. It's like an asteroid. I'd have it cut off if it was mine.

I have to clench my teeth. My stomach hurts, my arm is going numb. I feel like I'm being shut in a door. We go twenty yards, up the street, down the street. How do you tell which is which?

Right on cue David steps out of a doorway, slams the nearest dingo in the crutch with his boot. As the guy doubles up, for even lilies have balls, an elbow crunches his nose. There's a sound like breaking toffee. A knee follows the elbow home, smashes the cartilage to bits, twice. A third time for luck.

I start grappling with my guy. I try to head-butt him the way I've seen people do. But I can't get near his damn face. He tries to knee me in the crutch. We hop around like a couple of drunks. This is what real street fighting's like; none of your John Wayne stuff.

We stumble over each other's feet. A *pas de deux* for madmen. I land on top of him, sink my teeth into his blotchy cheek. His stubble nearly flays me. Behind me I can hear the other bull smashing his way through a plate-glass window. Somebody's going to be bloody annoyed about that.

The guy lets go of my crutch to prise my teeth out. I scramble up, spit out a lump of flesh, try to kick him in the head. I swing with everything I've got, give my best Gurkha yell. But my stupid toe catches the ground and I fall on his chest with a shriek. He pummels me off. I'm starting to get the worst of it, blood's beginning to spurt out of my nose.

David steps in. Christ knows where I'd be without him. A well-polished boot lams the lawman's ear half off. But he gets up, staggers into a shop doorway, whips out Mr Grossman's gun. He levels it at my chest. I twist away with a yell, but there's no place to go!

Poom! The goddamn gun explodes! The guy spins to one side howling, splashing flecks of blood in all directions. Amazing! I gawp at him! But David grabs me, shoves me away. I try to run. But it's one of my weaker efforts. My ankle's screaming. He drags me by the collar.

'He's still got my bloody krugerrand!' I cry.

But I should worry. You should see the blood on David's shirt. He looks really annoyed, it was almost brand new. He's annoyed with me too. He told me not to try flogging it.

And that's how it bloody goes. I've lost again. The whole thing was a waste of flaming time. I might as well not bother having any more good ideas. Just another useless adventure. What the hell is the point of it all? I ask myself. I always end up with less than I bloody started with. Why does it happen, all the time, on and on without respite? I don't know. I think I'm bloody cursed. I'm doomed, aren't I? I'm bloody doomed. And now even David's narked with me.

TWELVE

Now I stand in the badlands called Junk City. An alien and macabre place. A memorial to a fugacious world. A land where scrap metal comes to die. A necropolis for transportation. One more dustbin for the fly-by-night toys of man.

Huge metal towers rear like the Babel of a lunatic or a devil's bejewelled fingers, tarnished from the things he's been dipping them in. Glittering, nictitating in the sun and the rain. Singing as the head-shaking wind zips through. Waiting. Pondering. Brooding on their lot. Thinking their metallic thoughts; dreams of coupling with fuel nozzles, of chrome and vinyl and engines that start.

As the turmoil of the dump's establishment subsided, people pussyfooted in. Eerie people. Vagrants and junkies, the dispossessed and the disaffected. The unbalanced and the unbridled. People too mean to attain a state of poverty. The sick and the dead. They called it Megalopolis. Junk City. JC. An automaniac's heaven. You can collect the autographs of a dead species. You can cut your wrists open on the jagged fender of a Mercedes or a Colt. You can kick the wheel off a dustcart or a plane. You can throw yourself off the top of a mountain; bury yourself in tyres.

The towers must be seven or eight hundred feet high. There must be ten or twelve of them; it's hard to say, some are hidden in mist. You couldn't count the cars, there must be millions of them. So much rust you could powder it down and make a beach.

The air around plays doloroso. The air around stinks of urine and metal, of plastic, oil and rotting dogflesh. It hums with flies. Rats count the humans to see who's winning. If you have a chest complaint, stay away. If you're unsteady on your feet you'll break your neck. The garden of Junk City is a minefield, it's an incontinent crop of toxicating ooze and raff, of venomous razor-edges and sly false-footings. A club and fang world.

The sun has been swallowed by an amoebic cloud. Too slow, it lost its way across the sky. Ran out of steam. Ran out of nerve. I light a cigarette, pin the scene. The smoke pokes a finger in my eye.

'This is the closest I've ever been,' says David.

I blink hard to clear my eye. 'It's a lot closer than I've been. I've only seen it in the distance.' On my trip to watch Franklyn's spectacular death. I wonder if there are any bits of him still about? A tooth maybe. A length of tibia.

'Looks like a great place for kids.'

'Yeah.' Lousy place for grown-ups. Especially this one.

A little chapel stands alone amongst the waste land. I don't know how it has survived. It's a sort of miracle I guess.

We sat on the guanoed steps and chewed our lunch. It wasn't much of a lunch; half a packet of stale cornflakes and a pilfered apple. But then, it isn't that much of a chapel. All the windows are steeled over and there's graffiti on the walls. 'God hates Jews', that kind of thing. But the place still stands, grey and solemn, full of pigeons. I don't think there are services there any

166

more. It's just a landmark. A gnome in this garden of megaliths. A place for people to eat their cornflakes.

I hope there isn't a God. If there is, He must be very disappointed when He looks around a spot like this. He must wonder, if this is the best they can come up with after all those millions of years, whether it was all worth it. I wonder if He blames Himself? I wonder if He became bored long ago and wandered away to begin again elsewhere. What's the point in hanging around? What have we got to offer Him now?

Does He really care what we think? Does it really matter to Him whether folk believe in Him or not? A mind full of idle questions. A belly full of wind.

If it only took Him seven days to create it all, those creeping years since must seem like an eternity. Perhaps He's always had a sneaking hope that the ants would come out on top. Perhaps those big nests that wood ants build are really churches.

The patience of a saint must be nothing compared with that of a god. And at least saints have something to aim at. But where does a god go? Maybe there are supergods. Maybe He's moved up. It's hard to put yourself into God's mind. It's hard to put yourself in anyone's mind. I mean, I don't know why David does the things he does. I don't know why I do the things I do.

Maybe God doesn't.

THIRTEEN

There are reckoned to be several hundred people living in the tangle of Junk City. On dark nights it's said to light up like a Christmas tree. (Must be said by someone with a good memory, Christmas trees don't light up these days. No one can afford it. No one can afford Christmas. Most people eat a pigeon for their dinner.) You'd think with all those people about it would be easy to find someone.

Is it buggery! We wandered around all afternoon and the only time we saw anyone was when we stood in front of a tinted windscreen. We could have been archaeologists.

As darkness dripped through the holes in the sky we gave up. We were really in a fell mood. We hadn't been talking to each other for about four hours. Sulking. It was a night when the stars were as bright as a fairy's toenails on party night and the sky was three shades of blue.

But we were not in a mood to rhapsodize about it. We crawled into the cab of an old lorry and chewed on bent cigarettes. We didn't say anything. I fell asleep pretty pronto. I had a dream about running after someone who didn't want to talk to me. He was so intent on ignoring me, in the end he fell into a hole in the ground. And I stood at the top wondering who he was and where he'd gone. My life is full of questions like that. I never know what's going on.

When I woke up, daybreak and some, David had gone. That's good isn't it? What the hell did I do now? Should I go or should I stay? Had he gone for a slash or had he been abducted by androgynous aliens? I tried to move but my back had gone into rigor mortis. I had to unpeel myself from the toes up. It was hot in the cab and my head was busting. I'm suffering a lot with headaches these days. It may be that my brain is trying to escape.

I sat and stared dully out of the fragmented windscreen. It was a dull scene. There was morning mist. Morning chill. I opened a door to let some of it into the cab. Morning stillness. I staggered out for a hiss, hauled myself back in, propped my feet up, rolled a skinny fag. I ate the last few cornflakes. That didn't take long, there were only seven. How long is that likely to last me? I tried to ignore my heartburn. My heartburn which gets more like a furnace every day.

I watched the sun grow bright as it pared away the mist. Shadows stirred themselves, came out for a stretch. Something that looked a lot like a head louse fell on to my shirt. That's all I need. I had crabs when I was on the Canal and it took me bloody months to get rid of them. I tried to crush it but it kept on kicking, so I frizzed it with my butt. My head started to itch all over.

David didn't come back. A boring half hour sighed and yawned by. I cleaned my teeth with a match and my gums bled. I cleared some wax from my ears and they began to buzz.

I blinked because I thought my eyes were going funny. But it wasn't my eyes. There were things moving in the rubbish that litters the scene. For everything comes to hungry, convenient Junk City. It's one huge dump. Refuse is attracted like VD to a brothel. It's spreading into the surrounding areas like a cancer. They're going to have to burn it down one day.

Hunched-over things, like grey, browsing cattle. I sat up to get a better look. I couldn't figure it for a while. There were a couple of dozen of them. They just seemed to rise up out of the ground. Silent as the dead. Shuffling, shambling like run-down clockwork apes. I suddenly realized what it was all about.

It was the start of a strange exercise. And kind of frightening. Someone dripped ice cubes down my spine.

It was children, searching for their breakfast. Looking for their food, in the filth that other people throw away.

Things went from creepy to worse. An hour or two later, somebody screamed. And not just a 'let's have a scream' scream. This was the real McCoy, straight out of a horror movie. The kind of noise that makes mincemeat of your nerves and spits your guts out a mouthful at a time. It went on and on. It sounded as if a scream itself was being tortured.

God, if I'd had a pot of Valium then I'd have been shoving them in every orifice. I was rigid. Stiff as a teenager's erection. I had a feeling something awful was about to happen. Probably to me.

That's the trouble with paranoia. I'd be better if I was an agoraphobic or somesuch. What is that, fear of fields or something? I don't know. I've probably got it anyway. I think I've got bloody everything.

I've got so many phobias, I'm running out of places to keep them. Phobias, neuroses, I'm a psychological flypaper. I'm so paranoid I'm scared to look behind in case somebody jumps on me from in front.

I remembered to extricate my gun and shook some of my pocket-muck out of the barrel. It was a fairly new one, but already it had the shakes. Even my gun needed a trank. I prised my teeth apart. Nobody was about; the scavengers had faded away a little while back. One moment they were rooting about, next thing, they'd vanished. Eerie man. My ears nearly tore themselves off my head, straining for sounds. What did I hear? Nothing. A few gulls.

The scream started up again, triggering anew all the prickles in my body. It made me lift out of the seat. It was a scream and a moan now, a sort of 'aoowohhwah'. But right at the top of the skull. I thought perhaps someone had been pulled down by dogs. But I'd have heard them. Perhaps someone's being torn to bits by dogs with laryngitis? Maybe it's rats, there are some damn monsters around here. Christ I wish I knew what was going on. It doesn't sound all that far away. Where the hell is David?

I peered out cautiously. Like so cautiously you'd have fallen asleep watching me. Looked in as many directions as I could. Nothing. Just the bulk of the metal mountain behind me, another one right alongside with just a narrow, darksome defile separating them. That was to my right. Ahead of me my vision ran away to a hazy distance, a scene littered with the rusting junk of decades: drums, cans, plastic, glass. To the left a spur of burned-out twisted buses or something stabbed into my field of view like a skeletal finger. Above me, just a white sky, turning blue at the edges.

Nothing. When you're a coward you don't do anything to attract attention. Especially when there are screams up for grabs. So I stayed put and wondered if I could risk the click of setting the pistol. I'd probably shoot myself the way my hands were shivering.

A minute passed. The only sounds were mine, shuffling about in the cab, my clothes rustling, whispering to themselves. Then a third scream. More resigned now. A touch of anger, a shade of despair. Couldn't be dogs, people don't last that long. A faint shout – what was it, a cheer? I squatted down further. Not easy, I was already kneeling on the floor. I didn't know which way to look. When you're scared, danger always seems to be behind you. It was a mistake to put both eyes at the front.

I needed a wash. I seemed to be slimy with sweat.

Voices. I ducked down. Then I sneaked an eye up again – I had to know what was going on. Four hombres. All in their twenties or younger, dirty, ugly. One might have been half-caste. Half Sino maybe.

They were laughing. Obviously they hadn't been doing the screaming. One of them had a hammer in his belt. Cabinet-makers? Seemed unlikely.

I let them pass. I'm sure they appreciated that. They disappeared round the spur of buses. A silence followed them. Then the screaming voice took up again. 'Oh God!' it cried. 'Oh God!'

I waited for maybe a quarter of an hour. The voice had given up by then. God wasn't answering. But now there was something worse than that scream. Worse than the agonized lament.

Curiosity.

I fought it, God how I fought it. But it was no good, it was beating me. I just had to know. Chances are there was nothing to see. But I still had to find out. Curiosity. This is how pussies wind up hung from lampstandards with their paws hacked off. This is how kids come to find themselves dying in dark buildings at the hands of sweet-talking perverts. But what if it's David? It didn't sound like him, but screams have strange voices.

I ooze out of the cab. I hop from shadow to shadow, my pistol handy, my gaze spinning like a top. I creep through the dank, gloomy canyon where piles of ordure fester and rats chitter over a dead dog that the carrion kids have missed. Every so often I put my food down in a pool of sewage. It runs in at the lace holes. If I'm not sick in the next ten yards it's because I haven't had enough to eat.

I emerge into daylight. A few hundred yards away four towers, in a line, look as though they're about to set off on a march, but don't know which way to head. A fire smoulders, the smoke of old mattresses sniffs across the ground like a chimeric cat. Somebody moves, a distance away, disappears. Hard to believe this is still London.

Centre stage, thirty yards away, a middle-aged Negro, sobbing. Well he might. The poor sod has just been crucified.

On a wooden cross, he's in a classic pose. The hands are transfixed by nails, the wrists have been lashed to the wood to hold his weight. One leg is angled, a nail pins the foot to the frame. The other limb dangles free, waving about like a blinded animal.

He's in agony. Already his weight is driving the nail up his foot. His left leg snakes about, looking for support. But there's nothing there, only the heel of his nailed foot. And when he rests there his foot slides down the nail. The head of it has been bent over sideways so that he can't kick free. Either way, he loses. The pain is winning hand over fist.

His face is a study of agony. An artist would sell his soul for that look. Sweat percolates from the skin. The sweat of desperation. He's struggling to hold himself up. If he slumps, he's had it. I don't know too much about it, but I think you die of suffocation. When you pass a certain point, the scapulas press into the lungs and you can't inhale. Something like that. So the guy looks to be wrestling an invisible foe who's pushed his arms backwards. His torso slides inexorably forward, then he wriggles back. The thews of his neck threaten to burst the skin. Every movement makes the wounds grow larger, every heartbeat makes the blood run thicker. He's biting the end of his tongue off, but he doesn't realize it. The blood is dripping from his big toe.

Weirdest thing of all, the guy's got an erection.

The cross is about ten feet high. His feet are four from the ground. There are no ladders or anything, nothing to stand on. They must have nailed him to the frame, then hoisted it aloft. He's stopped screaming now, he doesn't have the breath. How long has he been up there? Half an hour or so. God, what will he be like after an hour? How long will he last – hours, a day maybe.

It's horrifying. And there's nobody about. He's dying this dreadful death alone. He's giving it everything he's got, putting a life into every bloody moment. And nobody even cares.

What the hell difference does it make anyway? Why should I care, he's nothing to me. The guy's dead anyway.

I look around to see if there's something I can stand on. I creep forward charily. Every eye is peeled, every ear stands on a stalk.

'Are you all right?' What a fucking stupid thing to say! Honest to God, sometimes you're just – you're just bloody stupid.

The bozo sees me through his crinkled eyes. His teeth are nearly embedded in each other, they're cracking in his torment. He's frothing, his nose and mouth are a mess of slime, like a bucket of slugs has exploded. He struggles up again. He's a heavy guy, he must be thirteen, fourteen stone.

'I want – I want a shit,' he says.

I don't know how he can keep from going. And the next second he can't, it comes out in a great dollop all down his leg. Horrible stuff, green and runny. God, there's no dignity in this kind of death. All the paintings in all those fancy galleries – they don't show you this. The smell of it burns up my nostrils. Junkie's shit. I have to step back. His erection subsides.

'If I can get up there, I'll get you down.'

He shakes his head. He can't hear me. He doesn't care a damn what I'm saying. Probably thinks I've come to throw stuff at him. People do that; they throw darts; they try to hit the nipples.

What to stand on though? Nothing to support me, nothing high enough. Perhaps they picked this spot because of that. I even contemplate shooting the man – his groans are becoming hideous. But I don't think I could do it. I wonder if Jesus made a lot of noise when he was on the cross?

I can't get the cross down, it's planted in a concrete pit. I'm starting to sweat myself. I look up at the frame. It's peppered with holes. This guy isn't the first. God, I wish there was someone else here.

I spin around at a sound. There is.

Three of them. Two of the bazonkas I saw earlier. And a new face. A face set a long way off the ground, and grinning like a wolf. This is the biggest bald mulatto I've ever seen. The people I bump into seem to be getting taller and taller. Whatever happened to the Harrys and the Franklyns?

They're all three grinning. But I don't feel like smirking back. They look the sort of folk who'd like to rape nuns. One glance was sufficient. I ran.

They caught me in less than fifty yards. Not one of history's great hegiras. I couldn't even make a fight of it, I dropped the gun when I bolted. One of them gave it back to me. Butt first, right in the gonion.

God I hate being hit. But being kicked is even worse. I got one in the tushes, one in the ear, one in the belly, a few in the back, a couple in the crutch. My bottom lip ripped apart, my cheek split, I was almost circumcized. There was a drumlike throbbing in my ears.

I crawled along the ground a way dribbling blood and snot. I have a lot of style. My balls were throbbing like oranges in an automatic peeler. Then something kicked me in the ear and I lurched into darkness, groaning.

FOURTEEN

Later, it's still dark. But not so black as it was earlier in the day. Earlier I thought I was probably going to die. Earlier I was thinking death might be a blessing.

When I recovered from my beating I was face to face with the insane Marko, leader of the Crucifixion Squad. Pontius Pilate. The madman. I was more face to boot, since I was on the deck and he was standing over me. It looked the sort of boot that had kicked a lot of faces to bits, a steel-capped combat boot, scuffed and rutted and polished with the blood of broken noses.

Hold your breath and I'll tell you how they woke me up. Someone pissed on my face. I've had some pretty disgusting things happen to me in my time, but that one won by a street. I woke in a gale of cachination, to see this little shit flipping his cock away and zipping up. He thought it was a great laugh. I rubbed my sleeves across my face and tried not to cry. That was about all the movement I could manage; I was throbbing all over.

The boot ground the dirt in front of me. Gradually the horselaughter subsided. I lifted my face from the floor and tried to get my bearings. I got as far as a kneecap. My arms were trembling with the effort of supporting me.

I looked around, saw quite a crowd of holes and stoppers, the mulo among them. My eyes were pounding like angry boils. A lot of murmuring fluttered

177

in my ears, commingled with the singing that the kicking had planted. I wondered how many broken ribs I had. A chestful I decided. But I was wrong, I didn't have any. I tried to suck in enough breath to cough out the mucus in my throat but I couldn't get my lungs past the first notch. My left hand was swollen like an arctic mitten.

'Hey!' The voice came from above the knee. 'Hey! Pissead!' All the cohorts fell about at that. A bunch of yes men. I squinted up, just about turning my neck through the stiffness that was trying to cripple it. A face was grinning down at me. 'Do you know me?'

I nodded. The face turned to the laughing onlookers. 'Hey, he knows me! I'm famous! I'm a star!' More of that stupid, abrasive laughter. God, Christ, there's nothing like phoney laughter for setting your teeth on edge. I felt bile rising up my escalator, tried not to retch.

The face loomed down on me like a vulture. 'Hey! Do you know my name? Do you know my name? What's my name?'

I squeezed some saliva into my mouth. It was too dry to make a sound. 'What's my name?'

'Marko,' I croaked.

'What?' he shouted, meaning I hadn't said it loud enough.

'Marko.'

'Heyyy!' He brayed again, turning to the pack. 'What's my *other* name?'

'P –,' I couldn't get enough breath. 'Pilate.'

'Yeah!' he said triumphantly. 'The Crucifier!' He did a kind of little war dance. 'The Cru-ci-fi-*yer*!' He's frigging insane. God, I stink of piss.

My senses were coming back to me now, pushing a

way through all the aches and spears. I was in a dark room. The walls were lined with squares of plyboard or something and painted green. There was dirty sand on the floor, full of butts and matches and balls of muck, chewing gum and phlegm. There were chairs leaning about, rickety and sagging, a couple of tattered sofas spewing their guts. A couple of tables, loaded with ashtrays and candles and packs of cards. Porno mags were stacked a hundred deep. A couple of bare light bulbs dangled from the ceiling, breathing out a sick yellow light.

Standing about, on the floor, the sofas, eighteen, twenty people. A piece of sacking covered one of the doors, the door to outside, there was bright silver light beyond and more folk talking and laughing. Other openings, with no doors; just dark passages behind them. Tunnels to hell. A rest home it wasn't.

Marko was leaning over me again. His spittle was sparking on my face. 'You like to see them stuck up, do you? You like to see them stuck up?' He wasn't laughing now. He was hissing. He gave me time to answer, which I didn't. 'You were gonna take him down, weren't you?' I shook my head. I thought he was going to slam me in the face, I was already wincing. 'You were gonna pull the bastard off!' I shook my head again.

'You shoulda kept your nose out, Pissead. You shoulda punched his stinkin' legs! You know what? You gonna see what it's like boy! You gonna see what it's like!'

Before I had a chance even to think about making a move a couple of them had me by the arms, pulling me up backwards. I started to yell. Marko was roaring again now, there was an ominous glassiness about his

179

eyes, like he was focusing on a point beyond my face, a point that only he could see. 'Ahahahaha!' like a machine gun. 'Ahahahaha!' I began to kick and thrash. They pulled me out through the sacking. 'Hey! Hey!'

A terrible panic gripped me then, as I watched the squad spill out of the sacking behind me, shrieking, shouting. Blonde-haired girls, tight-cropped Negresses, tattoos, swastikas, daggers, combat boots. 'Ha ha ha! Ha ha ha!'

They dragged me backwards across the rubble, and pretty fast too, my heels were bouncing, scrabbling for purchase. They were nearly dislocating my shoulders. 'Hey! Hey!' Jesus Christ, they were going to crucify me! Jesus Christ!! I struggled like I'd gone bloody berserk, I was nearly tearing my arms out to get away; but they had me fast, I couldn't get anywhere. I started snorting, snarling, they must have thought they had hold of a dog. But you're not suddenly bestowed with superhuman strength, I was battling uselessly. 'Let go of me you fucking bastards! Help! Help!'

My cries rang into the deaf ears of Junk City and died. 'Jesus Christ Almighty! Heelp! Heeelp!!'

The afternoon sun bent down for a closer look. The air was so thick you could tie it in knots. There was a sickness boiling up in my guts, I was panting like I was trying to pump it up. 'Ah Jesus, Jesus!'

They hauled me fifty, sixty yards. On the ground a stout wooden cross of dark wood lay soaking up the sun, one arm pointing at me like an accusatory shadow. It had been employed before, I was just another victim, just another slow death. 'No! Nooooh!' Two guys and one of the girls tugged it into a better position so that it was flat on the ground. A circle gathered, thirty or forty maybe; I couldn't see too clearly, my vision was in

180

a whirlwind. Again and again I threw myself against the restraining arms, but I could have been butting a bastion. I couldn't even see the bastards gripping me. I was pounding thin air.

A little gazebo appeared in front of me, hopping around the crowd, showing them the nails. There was a seven-pound hammer dangling from his belt. Oh Jesus Christ Almighty, this is unreal! I flung myself again, ripping the sinews in my shoulders.

Suddenly they yanked me back, jerked me off my feet. I crashed down, nearly smashing my spine on the main beam of the cross. I bucked, twisted, tried to claw myself off it, but half a dozen hands had me pinned down. I started to scream. Their hands were crushing me, gripping like pliers as they flattened me to the wood. Someone brought out lengths of red plastic string, lashed my wrists and ankles to the wood. They were shouting and cheering, but all I could hear were my own roars. My bladder puked.

The little bastard danced into my field of vision, leering. He's insane, you can see it in his eyes. And he really hates blokes bigger than him. He's probably a frustrated lesbian or something. I crawled into the wood, as far as I could go, shrieking within my skin, weeping out of the terror of my eyes and my throat.

You'd think there'd be something you could do when someone's about to torture you – but there's nothing. You can't scream yourself free, you can't tear yourself loose – you're just useless. And you can thrash and clench and spit and snarl, but at the end of the day, you're still the loser. You're still impaled. You still pump blood. At the end of the day, you're still an animal roaring in pain. At the end of the day, you're

dead. And maybe you just get a glimpse of a thought –
that your life really is not your own, but belongs
to whatever vicious bastard wants to take it from
you.

I screamed. God, I screamed.

I screamed as the nail drew blood from my palm. I
screamed as the hammer hung in the air like an anvil
about to crush me. God, how I screamed when the
hammer came whistling, winging, sickening down –
and the shit lurched into my pants.

And the wood of the cross bounced under the force
of the blow. I wailed. But not for the pain. They were
hooting. The anvil had landed close to my fingertips.
It hadn't touched me at all. They were all hooting. It
was a joke. A joke. Just a rotten, stinking, bastard joke.
They were falling about. Jesus Christ. Jesus Christ. . . .

It took me an hour to stop jerking.

That was Marko's gag. What a great laugh we'll have
about that one day, hey? I hope he gets cancer of the
bollocks. I hope his spleen explodes.

That was his jest. He showed me a picture of myself,
one of the early 'wanted' posters, after Leighton
Buzzard. 'See!' he bellowed with idiotic mirth. 'We
knew who you was all along! Four of my women, they
got away from that shithole! You really fucked 'em up
good hey? Four of my chicks! See! See! It's a joke, it's a
big joke! We big buddies! I owe you man! I owe you!
You great guy!'

Ha ha. I grinned weakly. Like the shagged-out,
puked-up nerve-wreck I felt, and another riffle took
over my body for a minute. 'Ahahahahaha!' His
machine-gun laugh blasted me. 'Ahahahahaha! Hey!

Hey! Fuckin' good joke hey! Fuckin' good laugh! You like it? You like it?'

I nodded. 'Fucking good laugh,' I murmured.

'Ahahahahaha!' He slapped me a stinging one on the cheek to show what good buddies we were, stomped off on an enormous, acrid fart. He must eat offal. I indulged in a quiet relph, though there was little but a spoonful of slime to bring up. I brought it up anyway.

That was this afternoon. Now it is late evening, the time when the clocks start darkening the sky. The time when virginity trembles. Outside stars are burning their pinprick holes in the mantle yet again. Inside, in the green room where I lay numbering my hurts, my contusions, the two yellow bulbs keep twilight lingering on. It's a big room. There must be fifty people in it, the nucleus of Marko's squad. The Warriors.

Marko is there, the psychotic warlord. He never misses a chance. When some kid brought in a trapped gull, its legs tethered to a length of cord, it was Marko who blasted it to a bloody Kingdom Come with a Colt 45. Man, that is a mean bastard of a gun. Some handguns, they look like cigarette lighters; a Colt 45 is a Gun. The boom in that crowded chamber nearly sent the whole of my stomach pitching out of the small of my back. The bird was sent ten feet across the room. Its final flight. It all but disintegrated.

The black girl next to me sniffed on some snow and sighed. 'He's frigging nuts.'

'Who – Marko?' I whispered.

'Yeah. He's a fuckin' screwball.'

'I guess that's why he's the boss hey?'

Her eyebrows shrugged. She passed me a joint. She was a good-looking chunk of ladyhood. About five-four, tight, clean, about the only one who didn't look as though she'd got some form of venereal disease. 'You wanna screw?'

'Er . . .' Pretty forthright too. What does one say? 'Er – what, here? Now?'

She shrugged her shoulders. As far as I could tell she hadn't even looked at me yet, she was just watching people play cards, pick their teeth, watch the boob. 'I don't mind,' she shrugged again.

It was a – well, exciting offer. I've never, sort of, had it offered like that before. And, to be honest, I fancied her like hell. I'd been watching her bum all evening. Trouble is, it's just not the way it's done, is it? I mean, is it? 'Just say if you don't want to, it's all the same to me.'

Not to me it isn't. I haven't had sex since – when did I last have sex? Aunty Mel. That isn't sex, it's a bloody rodeo. I carefully flexed all my aching, bruised muscles. I didn't want to seize up in the middle. 'Okay. Do you, er, have a room or something?'

'What do you think this is, a fuckin' hotel?' I noticed that quite a few folk were starting to make out on the floor in front of us. I couldn't do that. 'I got a bed,' she said impatiently, still not looking at me. 'You wanna make it there, or you wanna go across the other side of bleedin' London?'

We went to the bed.

The bed was the back seat of a Ford Granada. A Ghia, no less. In the front she kept a few clothes, make-up, vibrators, a hatchet, sanitary towels. She climbed in ahead of me, that beautiful tight bum was inches from me like the landscape of a promised land. She settled down in the far corner, began undoing buttons. Then she became thoughtful. 'I could have been a nun you know. Sister Thérèse Angelique.'

'Is that your name?'

'No, it's Cheryl. But I could have called myself that, if I was a nun.'

'So how come you ended up in the squad? This place isn't much like a convent.'

She ignored the question as she tried to kick her boots off. I knew the answer anyway. I've always wanted to lead a peaceful life and go to America. So how come I'm in the squad? Aye, life doesn't take a deal of notice of what you want. And we don't understand most of our own reasons anyway. Cheryl wriggled her shirt off. She sighed. She must have been tuning in to my ruminations. 'It's all the fuckin' same isn't it? Some people think JC is a shithole. You shoulda seen the place I was at before.'

'Doesn't anybody live in the heaps themselves?' The green room earlier, the Granada now, they were both underground. We were in tunnels beneath one of the metal buttes. 'I thought that's where everyone lived.'

She nodded. 'Yeah, a lot of people live up there. You don't see them much. They're pretty strange.' She laughed. 'This is like, upper class down here!'

'What about the cholera, doesn't that frighten you?' It frightens me. I haven't had anything to eat all day, I've only had alcohol to drink.

She laughed again, an oddly mirthless sound. 'I run with the Pilates and you think I should be scared of a bug! What the hell? Cholera today, the fuckin' plague tomorrow! There's always something, what the hell difference? D'you wanna bit of pokey or what, we gonna discuss like the social climate all night?'

I acquiesced, pulled my shirt off. She eased down her jeans, spread herself into a more receptive position. Good job I got myself cleaned up. She was attractive

185

you know, I don't think I could make it with someone I didn't fancy.

Trouble is, I couldn't make it this time either. The spirit was willing enough. . . . 'What's wrong with it?' she said, after about ten minutes, and she poked it a couple of times with her fingertips. I was after a ramrod and all I had was a rawlplug.

'I don't know. It's not 'cos I don't want to.' God, how humiliating.

'Well that fuckin' thing sure as hell don't want to! Has it ever been out on its own before?' After a minute she tutted, leaned into the front seat, produced a pack of fags. 'It's talking does it you know. You shouldn't never talk until you're started.' She didn't seem overly concerned. I was. I wanted to crawl through the floor. Twenty-nine and I'm bloody impotent. The beginning of the end.

We had a smoke, locked the doors, eventually dropped off the edge of sleep. I forgot the impotence somehow or other, went to sleep thinking of Homer. I could be close to the man now.

He could be close to me.

FIFTEEN

'Hey, Pissead! Pissead!' Someone was banging on the
window with a fistful of rings. 'Hey Pissead!' I
struggled to the surface. It was the mulo. He jerked his
head. 'Come on, we're goin' on a gig!'

I began pulling reluctant clothes on. It was stifling in
the Ford. It was broad daylight outside, but at the end
of the sloping tunnel where the car lay, it was dusky.
Cheryl stirred. 'Whas goin' on?'

'Some gig.'

'Oh fuckin' hell.' She turned over, followed the path
back to Morpheus.

'I'll see you later.' I clambered out, stooped below
the tangled metal talons which groped alarmingly into
the shallow gallery, tracked the mulo's footprints to the
squinting morning. The desolate butte reared up behind
me as I emerged, coughing, blinking, buckling my belt.
There were about a dozen dildoes slouching about,
couple of janeys amongst them. The mulo's tag is
Lewis.

I sneezed. 'Anything to eat?'

'Get something on the way.' Lewis proffered me a
smoke. Thanks a lot, pal. I suppose you think this makes
up for kicking the crap out of me. Just don't turn your
back when I've got an army with me. I coughed on the
draw, it was packed with dope. There was hardly any
room for tobacco.

Marko appeared. We set off. Strung out in a loose

187

bunch. I still didn't know what the hell was going on.

We walked for a couple of hours. There's a lot of perambulation these days. Greaseburgers for breakfast, cans of warm ale. It isn't hip to ask for a cup of tea. You can't be a man unless you burp.

We strode through the East End, strung out across the street in a loose wedge. People got out of our way. A few chicks made eyes. A few runts tagged behind. We turned into a side avenue, four-storey tennies watched us nervously. We stopped outside a blue one. A lad on the steps bolted indoors like he was on elastic. I guess this is the place.

Marko jerked his cranny – he hadn't spoken to me at all – I followed him inside with Lewis and two others. Into an aphotic passage. Dark faces peeped out at us, popped out of sight. We made our way through a succession of miasmas. Doors slammed.

Up a flight. Kids on the landing vanished. It wasn't getting any lighter. The air was so hot, so still, I expected to see condors sitting on the bannisters. Something bad was going to happen and there was no way I could avoid it. This was the path to the albino. If I strayed from it I was dead.

I was probably dead anyway. Up another flight. My heart followed one step behind, thumping like a sack of coal. Whatever was at the end wasn't going to be good.

On the topmost landing, the furthest portal. Lewis kicked it off the lock. A white gal tried to bolt past; one of the jerks stuck a hand in her way, caught her by the throat, shoved her back into the room. She only had a pair of knickers on. She landed in a heap on the lino. Christ, something bad was going to happen here. That girl had the look of a victim. I tried to steel myself.

We practically filled the goddamn room. Lewis

snaked the doll up, tucked her throat into the crook of his elbow. He's a massive git, she looked like a rag. I don't think he even noticed that she was battling like a tiger. Marko motioned the other two to wait outside. I'd have willingly swapped with one of them.

The apartment was rank. The stink of urine was enough to bleach your hair. On the crawling bed, amongst the bugs, a spade sprawled, barely conscious, arms a mass of puncture points. His face looked like it had been through two deaths. He was scared, man. Like he was really juddering. And too far gone to make a move.

'Where's my fuckin' stuff?' snarled Marko, and whoever the hell the guy on the bed is – I wouldn't swap places with *him* for the keys to heaven itself.

'I swear to God man, I was going to pay it back. Honest to Christ, Marko. Oh Jesus man, you know me, I was so strung out – this guy – I was only –'

Marko interrupted the babbling, his voice so low it seemed to hit you in the belly. 'Where's the fucking stuff, Deeko?'

'I swear to God man, I couldn't help it, oh Jesus Christ, oh Jesus Christ.' He burst into tears. He was too weak to even move off the bed.

'What did you do with it, Deeko?'

He didn't want to tell. He'd done something naughty and he didn't want to own up. He thrashed the bed in his desperation, his black skin lacquered with perspiration. 'Where's the goddamned shit, Deeko!' He shouted it that time, and it lashed the guy like a whip. Made me wince too. It's not a patient kind of voice.

'I don't know! I don't know! Oh Christ, Pilate, I don't know man, I don't know!' he wailed.

Marko motioned. Lewis thrust the girl forward, still

keeping the lock on her neck. 'What did he do with it?'

The girl was so scared she was blue. 'He s-s-s-sold it!' she dithered. 'Him and a c-c-c-c-c-c-couple of g-g-guys. The-the-they she-she-she-shot up!'

'What guys?'

'Re-Re-Re-Re-Rooney! Re-Rooney an' Ke-Ke-Capaldi!'

Marko turned to the bozo on the bed. 'She's a smart chick.' Then in a sudden move he whipped out a switchblade, stabbed it deep into the left side of the girl's round belly, sliced it straight across. The girl screamed, I vomited greaseburger, and her guts chased each other out all over the bed and the guy's feet. He screamed. Lewis threw her into the steaming mess, held her face in it, her hands clutched fistfuls of her own sticky viscera. She moaned, gargled on it.

They hauled the screaming Deeko up, dragged him to the window, butted the glass out with his face, bundled him out head first. He screamed for the first thirty-five feet. After that he was spewing blood on to the paved yard at the back. Marko and Lewis looked down curiously, then through the room's few possessions, the single wardrobe, the tiny dresser, a tatty bag under the bed. It took about thirty seconds. They found nothing of interest. Practically nothing at all. The girl was still groaning. She'd slumped to the floor, dragged all her guts on top of her.

We went out, downstairs. Marko banged on every door. 'Everybody out! Everybody in the street! This building's being torched!' They flooded out like lemmings. We followed them on to the street. Marko beckoned a dame over. 'Go find Capaldi and Rooney.' She minced off on a bum like ball bearings.

'Is everybody out?' Marko looked around. 'Go set

fire to the fucking place!' Two monkeys bounded up the steps, eager beavers, rattling matches. The rest of us stood around chatting, except I didn't say anything. The people from the building huddled in little clusters, waiting to see their possessions go up in smoke. Little clusters of frightened people. I was a frightened cluster all on my own.

After a few minutes we saw smoke wandering out of the ground-level windows. It looked around the scene for a moment, drifted up to have a gander over the roof. The eager beavers pranced out like a couple of tarts, flushed with their efforts. I hope they get syphilis of the lip.

The fume inspissated, gathered into a ball, cascaded skywards, the windows heaving, retching fit to bust. People in adjoining buildings, only just cognizing what was going on, became panicky. There was turmoil aplenty, smoke, squalls, the lingo of fracturing glass.

We lingered until the place was well ablaze, then departed. Another day gets underway. Another nightmare.

SIXTEEN

The whole incident left me pretty numb. Two people had been killed, a lot of homes charcoaled and I didn't even know why. Obviously some perfidy was involved. But the consequences were appalling. You should have seen that black guy's eyes when the girl's guts spilled on his feet. You should have heard him scream.

For a couple of hours I didn't talk to anybody. Not that they noticed, they were all stoned to the tits. There are more drugs around here than I saw in the hospital. Seems if I was going to stay in Marko's squad much longer, I was going to have to become a mainliner myself. I don't mind burning the odd bush, but these wallies have darts coming out of their goddamn eyeballs.

By mid-afternoon most of them are senseless and I'm sitting next to Cherry, who still seems fairly level. We share a smoke. I take a deep breath. I figure time is running out for me. I'm not going to last long in this bunch. I didn't like the way Marko looked at me when I threw up. That's probably why he took me up to Deeko's pad. There's no room for faint-hearts. I take the plunge. 'Do you know an albino guy called Homer?'

'Homer?' she snorted smoke like a dragon. 'That fuckin' psycho!' Sounds like she knows him. 'Fuckin' crazy bastard shit all over me once!' Good heavens. I wonder why he did that?

'Does he hang out here much?'

'What do you want him for? You're best to keep out of his way. He's a fuckin' psycho!' So you said.

'I used to know him, before he was quite so psycho. I owe him something.'

'If he'd of wanted it back he'd of got it. I wouldn't go near him in a – tank!'

'Does he stay here, in the camp?'

'Nah.' She topped up her cup of wine with vodka, twitched her head. 'Stays up there. With the weirdoes. Which is what he is!'

'When was the last time you saw him?'

'You sound like a fuckin' sheriff! What time is it now? About three hours ago.'

Three hours ago! Holy shite! 'You mean he's here now!'

'He's gone again now. He came looking for Marko, but you was all out. Christ that guy's a bloody – a bloody –'

'Psycho?'

'Yeah.'

'When's he coming back?'

'I don't know. He's a nutter. I hope he never comes back.'

I pulled my jacket from under me, took the new pistol out, stuck it in my belt. Homer. Three hours ago I could have killed him. Or he could have killed me. If it came to a shootout there'd only be one outcome. And it wouldn't be me. I looked at Cherry, lying back in the sun now, her eyes closed. If I stuck close to her, maybe, if he comes, I could use her as a shield. . . .

Jesus Christ, what am I talking about? I rub my face in horror. Is this Beekay, this jiver talking about using a human shield? God Almighty man, when does the killing ever stop? When does it stop?

193

What will happen if I kill Homer? What will the squad do with me? Tommy said the albino had made a few hits for them – do they owe him anything? Maybe this wasn't such a good idea. Rather than picking off the spider, I just seem to be getting caught up in its web. Why do I only think so far?

Why the hell do they need Homer anyway, when there are sixty or seventy thugs here already? More than that, there's upward of a hundred in the squad altogether. Maybe it's a territorial thing. Perhaps, despite their power, they're pinned down by similar gangs all around. I don't know. I don't ken much of this violent hierarchy.

Maybe Homer doesn't work for them. Maybe they work for Homer. It's giving me a headache all this. It was simpler when I was a kid, you just had goodies and baddies. Now there are baddies and baddies, but none of them are quite the same. They all have slightly different roles. But they mesh together – like sewers running under the city – they undermine the whole of the society. It's attacked from above and it's attacked from below and there's just a thin line in the middle where right and wrong still mean something.

Problem is, I appear to have lost sight of it. Once you get into the darkness of the sewers, everything becomes confused.

Like Cheryl. I mean, she seems okay, I even fancy her – what is she doing in all this? Why isn't she in that middle band?

'Cherry?' She wakes up. 'What do you think of Marko?'

She yawns. Her teeth are pretty good. I envy them. 'He's okay. He comes a bit quick.'

Sex plays a prominent part in the life of a squad.

194

Mostly rape. 'What do you think about – like what went down this morning?'

'What, Deeko? What's there to think about? He fucked up, he got screwed.' She shrugged it off carelessly.

'But what about all the other people? The ones who lived in the building.'

'What about them? If you can't take it you go under.' She yawned. 'They're just jerks. They ain't worth a shit.' She pummelled her rolled-up shirt to make a better pillow. 'It'll be different when Haldane's the boss. We'll see some action then.'

Haldane? Leading light of the fascist movement, the National Party. I'd heard his name mentioned earlier. God, I thought the squads were, like apolitical. I didn't realize. . . .

'All the squads – do they all follow Haldane?'

'"Follow" him? We don't follow him man, he isn't Bo Peep you know!'

'But they all want to see Haldane in control? I mean, would that, like, make a difference to them?'

'Who the hell else is there?' She closed her eyes, emitted a dainty fart. One of those little high-pitched ones. I saw her in a new light then. I'm glad I didn't make it with her. I lay back myself. God. The web gets bigger and bigger and ever more complex. Fascists, the squads, Homer, the army. Who the hell is fighting for whom? It makes the Irish terrorists look like the good guys! God, how am I going to get out of this? Why the hell did I get into it!

I didn't know the squads were pro-fascist. It was bloody Marko's group who killed Mr Grossman, the Jew. I'd forgotten about that. Shit, I don't like this at all at all. I feel like a cat among the bloody wolves. God,

195

the more you learn the more you don't know. Brrr. All this kind of thing is putting years on me. No wonder my stomach hurts.

Where the hell is David? That's something else I don't know. I'm all on my greta. Homer might be around the next corner, and there's just me and a pistol that I haven't even fired yet. Just me. Maybe I should make a break for it. Maybe I should blow my own brains out and save Homer the trouble. Probably not, I'd probably miss. I'd probably blow my ear off.

I gave Cherry a dig to wake her. 'This Homer – which way does he come from, when he comes?'

She was narked. 'Oh God, how would I know! Any bloody way he likes! What d'you wan', a bleedin' fanfare?' I wouldn't mind.

She showed me her back then, settled down in a huff. I noticed that she had a lot of little bites on her neck and shoulders, like bugs. She gets less and less attractive all the time. I don't think I fit in with this gang life. One of the girls started throwing up. My head began to throb.

SEVENTEEN

The next day was quiet, which suited me fine. Life is too hectic by half for my liking. I just sat in the shade with a catapult, tried to hit rats. I didn't get any though. They're pretty smart those rats. One day they're going to start chucking things back.

I figure, what I'm going to do, is give it a week. If Homer hasn't showed by then, I'll split. I'll go to David's sister's, leave a message in case he shows there. Then I'll go out to Leighton Buzzard, get as much of the cash as I can carry, go round all the prisons, bribing folk until I find Harry. And then – I don't know. I'll think of something.

That's what I should have done in the first place. How many prisons are there? I don't know. I'll buy a bike or something to get me about. Yeah, that's what I should have done. Wasted too much time, farting about.

I ought to learn to shoot straight too. It's no good turning away at the last second, you wind up blasting clouds.

Then what? I get Harry out. Meet up with Dave. We find Rachel. Maybe I'll ask Sebastian if she'd like to come along. . . . Yeah, that sounds okay. Maybe we shouldn't go to the States. Maybe we should go to South America, open up a corned beef farm or something. I don't know how you get there though.

I wonder what we could do in the States? Seb's a

nurse, she'd be all right. David could be a homosexual bodyguard. Harry could be a driver. Rachel could carry on hooking. No, probably not with Harry there. What about me? What could I do?

Bloody hell, everyone can get fixed up with something except me. That's flaming good isn't it?

Weather's getting cooler. Autumn around the next bend. Soon be winter. That's typical of me, decide to go cycling round the blooming country just when winter's putting on its overcoat. My catapult elastic has just snapped. Sod it. I toss it over my shoulder. I just can't be bothered any more.

I sit alone. In a city of eight million people, I'm on my own. Nothing but enemies. Nothing but my own, morbid, miserable company. I wish I was more fun to be with.

EIGHTEEN

Two days quietly pass. They pass so quietly you have to strain to hear them. The days have caught a chill. The little baa-lamb clouds of summer have become grey and sullen sheep. They're spoiling for a fight. They're just waiting for a day to rain on.

That rotten buddy autumn, him with the cold steel hidden behind his back, is on his way for a natter. Poor old summer. Never learns. Soon as her back's turned, wallop! Right in the neck. Another betrayal by that misty-eyed lackey of winter.

There's a meeting. An EGM of the squad. The topic? Gang warfare. I attend. Everyone connected with the squad attends, a hundred and twenty or so. It's crisis time. The squad is shaky.

I'll fill you in on what I've learned about the gangs during the last couple of days.

Marko's squad ain't what it used to be. Defections. Betrayals. Isolation. They've all taken their toll.

A few years ago, when the squad was establishing itself, JC was a good place for an HQ. The area is honeycombed with tunnels, blind alleys; it's encompassed by open ground. From the top of the towers you can see anything coming for miles. The law could hunt for you for months.

But it takes a long time to get anywhere. Like it's a couple of hours to get into the city. You lose touch. You can't be bothered. The threat fades. You leave gaps for

199

others to plug. And they plugged them. Like Billy Bruce – who swears he's a direct descendant of Robert the Bruce. Even though he's black. Angel Face, another one.

Marko was hustled out. Unlike me, people weren't impressed by the crucifixions any more. Not when Billy Bruce disembowels folk, Angel shoves cylinder grenades up their fannies.

The final ignominy came when Marko's "lootenant", Marsha, defected to the Angels. From what I can see, she knows a sinking ship when she sees one. Marko has the haunted look of the hunted man. He's being squeezed out like a pimple. He's getting desperate.

There's only one way to go. He's going to take over Angel's territory. He's moving uptown. Trouble is, we're all expected to join in. It's always the sheep who end up in the butcher's.

That's what the Council is about. Today, so that there's no time for word to spill, we're going against the Angels. I joined this squad just in time didn't I?

The Angels of bloody Death.

It's almost time for me to split the scene, this isn't my kind of life. And God knows I'm tempted. Only one thing holds me back. After coming this far, and maybe getting so close – there's a chance that Homer will be in on today's caper. . . .

We drift into the area in dribs and drabs. Two here, one there. Odds and sods. Innocuous as hell. I reckon we look about as innocent as wolves with Bibles.

Some of us walk; some bike; some wait a couple of hours to chug in on the train. Just ordinary citizens. Nobody joes. Just mooching about. Except our pockets are stuffed full of grenades and bullets and we've got pieces of shotguns and machine guns shoved inside our jackets and down our trouser legs. I can hardly bloody walk.

It's about four o'clock. Six hours before the summer curfew. There's a drabness in the air. Summer senses something's wrong. The streets are full of dismal people. The sort of people who stand around staring at shrill, mindless brats. Shifty-eyed people, who look at you unaffably. Their faces look like hand-me-downs, like they've been slept in before. Their dowdy, weary houses fit them like jackets.

An abstract of their lives would run to two words. 'They lost.' But there's a sinister kind of patience about them. As though, one way or another, that's what awaits us all. It doesn't bring them any joy though. They look like they've just been wormed.

There's a commonplace hostelry on which we all descend. It's not a big joint, we practically cave the walls in as one by one we trickle in, two by two. The early locals choke on their flat ale, try to scuttle out of the doors. I don't blame them, we don't look like we're selling cockles.

But they're persuaded to stay. Quiet boys, don't blow the gaff. They huddle in a corner like a covey of virgins. The fat barman goes white then grey. He loses his voice completely, develops a frenetic nod, a nod so severe the sweat flies from the top of his pate like sparks.

Everyone sprawls about, slots their weapons together. I seem to have lost a bit of mine. I'm not very good at this, someone shows me how. Oh yeah; all of a sudden I'm holding a light-machine gun.

I adjust the crotch of my jeans. I had to sling the other

pair – they're not the same after you've crapped in them. These are a bit tight. I've got a sort of headband on to keep my hair out of my eyes. I pull it off, wipe my face with it. Hot in here. I take a long swig from a whisky bottle. Another. Brr, could do with more than whisky. Could do with a sick note from my mum. I check my pistol for the thousandth time, tuck it into my belt.

What the hell am I doing here? When I look around, all I see is violence. Violent dames, violent bucks. If you're not careful, you can get sucked into it. Forget reality.

Is this the reality though? These young girls with their cartridge belts, with their jeans tucked into dirty combat boots and their knives? The stubbly-chinned thugs with their bright headbands, gaudy tattoos? Is this the way we're headed? Christ, I don't know. It frightens me though. It frightens me that I'm a part of it, trying to make out on it for my own largely nebulous purposes.

Whose eyes am I looking through now? What am I feeling when things don't work out – conscience? Or disappointment? Where's the dividing line? Once you're a participant, it vanishes. You can only cross it once. It's like virginity.

'Does everybody know what they gotta do?' That's Marko. That's about the fifteenth goddamn time he's asked that. Everybody grunts, nods, breaks wind, looks up – 'What's that?' They're a bunch of dildoes. I pull my headband back on, wipe my palms on my jeans. What's there to know? You go in and shoot everything to hell. And if you're like me, you try to stick at the back and just shoot up doors and windows and things.

It's just another suicidal murder mission. One more chance to show your colours. Mine's a vivid yellow.

We were only a few hundred yards from Angel's place – a big old house, a huge place, upwards of forty rooms. It must have had servants, bell-pulls, chintz, crystal, all kinds of fancy stuff in its day. But no one could remember the day any longer. Now it's just a drab brown building turned over to the business of street warfare. The trophies in the gun-room are human lives, junkies, corpses, fatherless runts. Even the ghosts will have been scared off. A dowager old house, bereft of its former glory.

There are – one, two, three, four, five doors into the joint, two fire escapes. It must have been flats at one time, a hostel maybe. Most of the windows are boarded up, patched up one way or another. And the gutters are sagging; the place must stream water in the winter. Slates on the roof are creeping suicidally close to the edge.

Can't see it at the moment though. At the moment, we're knee-deep in shit and slime. At the moment, we're splashing our way through the goddamn sewers.

Gordon Bennett man, if I could have got away without being seen, I'd have gone. You wouldn't have seen my bum for dust. But by the time I realized what was going on it was too late. By the time I was *au fait* with the situation I was already being shoved into a square, stinking hole in the road. It was a drop of about eight feet. Eight feet, straight into a fetid stream that comes halfway up your shins. Straight into a river of goddamn lumpy sewage.

Oh God, this is awful. Hail Mary, full of grace. The

Lord is with you, you are blessed amongst women. And blessed is the fruit of your womb, Jesus. I would have crossed myself but I had to keep a hand on the wall to keep myself from falling, the underfooting was a slime like ice. The wall itself was just trickling with gunge.

Holy Mary, mother of God. Pray for me, a wicked sinner. Now and through the whole length of this godforsaken awful place. Please don't let me tumble into the stuff. Please don't let it soak up my jeans to my crutch.

The smell was like diarrhoea laced with acid. A searing, mordant, amaurotic thing. It bored through the back of my nose, tried to shove my writhing eyeballs out. The scarf wrapped around my face didn't help much – all it did was stifle my groans.

There were fifty, sixty of us, in a column, with a half-dozen torches flashing about nervously, looking for a way out. Bodies kept falling over, floundering in the filth. The place was falling down, dropping apart. The sewage was leaking away into the ground – no wonder there's so much typhoid – the roof was caving in. There were looming scuppers in the walls where thousands of rats clustered, gaping at the long beams of light like they thought it was God come to bless them. The constant drip dribble gurgle of water pouring in, bubbling out. The smell, God Almighty the smell. . . . It did everything but castrate you.

And they were the good bits. The turds piling against each other to form great floating islands on which rats crouched, the lumps nudging your legs in a horribly familiar way, the tatters of toilet paper that clung to your jeans like drowning men, the slime on the walls that conspired to wriggle down your sleeves – all that was something else again. That was the kind of stuff that made you want to put a bloody gun barrel in your mouth, that pushed you to the verymost brink of absolute hysteria.

And all around, a dreadful darkness. Behind the splashing, the cursing of the group – an eerie, watery delitescence. My sanity I think was clinging on by its nails. I wanted to slice off my skin with a carving knife.

Five more minutes and I'd open fire on everybody in front of me. I really would. I just couldn't take it. It was clamouring inside me, like if I didn't see some daylight soon I'd . . .

God, I could hardly be further away from America. What would my mother say if she could see me now? She probably wouldn't say anything, she'd just groan and collapse.

NINETEEN

We moved quickly. Down the street, blew away the couple of guards with stens, kicked open the doors, axed them aside. Bam bam bam bam bam!! down the corridors. Breaking glass, smashing woodwork. Kicking off doors, filling the rooms with the roar of guns and the heat of bullets. Bam bam bam bam bam!

I found myself with Lewis on the first floor. I still hadn't fired my gun yet. I hadn't seen anyone to shoot at to be honest, it was just a lot of noise and confusion. Lewis clicked another magazine into place, 'Come on!' He beckoned me with the gun and I went. I'm easy to command when I'm terrified. His face was bright with sweat. Mine must have looked like a soap powder advert.

A closed door. He looked at me. We clutched our guns a little tighter. Lewis flung himself against it – I'd have tossed a bloody grenade, but these macho guys love to get a few bruises. His massive shoulder demolished the wood in a dull explosion. Dum dum dum! A string of bullets ripped across his shoulder. Lewis pitched sideways, spitting blood. He looked really surprised. I dived to my right, dropped the machine gun, swung up my pistol, wincing.

Her gun had jammed. That was why I was alive. She glared at me panting, not a chance now, I had my gun trained right on her blanching lineaments. Her own gun slumped, useless. I'd won. 'Shoot her!' screamed Lewis. 'Shoot her!'

I knew who she was, though I'd never seen her before. She was the defector, Marsha. She had on a green combat outfit, a loose shirt, a gold chain round her neck. Her hair was brown, pushed loosely back on her head, but trying to spill forward. No make-up, tight, hard, aggressively female. Her dark eyes glared, waiting for me to kill her. Even at a moment like that the male in me thought – well, never mind that now.

'Kill her! Kill her! Kill the fucking bitch!' Lewis was scrabbling on the floor screaming at me. The whole of his side was crimson. It was all across his neck, his arms. He was in agony, furious. His gun was out of reach. He looked ugly as hell. He should've kept quiet.

If he hadn't said anything I might have shot her, out of fear. If she'd looked at the gun maybe, instead of my face. But he couldn't keep quiet. He had to scream out all his distorted, brutal animus. 'Shoot the bitch! Shoot her!' And I thought, why the hell should I, you bastard? I remembered the beating he'd given me. The boots in the crutch. His knuckles in my bloody mouth. Deeko's frightened girlfriend. But not this time Lewis, not this one.

I swung round and fired five booming slugs into his chest.

Lewis screamed for a moment before the blood gushing from his lungs filled his throat. Then it came pouring out of his nose and mouth. But he wasn't dead, he started kicking himself backwards with his heels, his white eyes rolling at me. A huge gout of blood, like a sac, burst out of his nose and hung across his lips. There was a grunting, strangling sound coming from his throat – but I don't know if he made it, or whether it was just the air finding ways to the surface.

He backed into the corner. Me and the girl just stood watching him. He must have gone insane or something. He pulled a knife and plunged it into his goddamn belly. And still he didn't flaming die! It was like a bloody nightmare! He started to drag himself up the frigging wall! His face was turning green!

God Almighty, I couldn't shoot him again, I just couldn't pull the trigger. I just watched horrified, wondering what the hell he was going to do next. He was almost upright, looking at me, with so much blood it was hard to see anything but red. Why the hell didn't he just die?

Then the girl moved. She picked up her gun by the barrel, swung it round her head with everything she had. It smashed into the side of Lewis's face, drove his skull against the wall, and the bone caved in with a muffled crunch. He crumbled. He slid to the deck. His head slumped forward between his knees. His blood dripped out thickly. He was still.

I couldn't speak. Marsha looked at me, all the colour gone from her face. The house was getting all shot to hell and we just stood there trembling like a couple of – I don't know, like guilty adulterers or something. She couldn't talk either. She tried to say something but nothing came out.

Finally I managed to jerk my head towards the door. 'Beat it darlin', before they catch you.' She didn't even take the gun with her, she just dropped it and fled. I staggered out of the room after her, my arms quivering like they were worked by batteries. I heard a scraping noise from the room behind me. It was Lewis's heels, kicking in the death throes.

*

And like my killing of Lewis, the raid itself was a disaster. It'd be bloody laughable if Marko wasn't walking just a few yards away. The place was almost empty. Half a dozen gazebos, no more. It was a cock-up. We'd waded through all the shit and nightmare for nothing. Angel wasn't there. He was out on a job. Burning the building down was somehow like an acknowledgement that we'd lost.

I didn't mind. Marsha was a better-looking lady than any we had on our side. It took me a while to get her out of my mind.

It wasn't really until Marko pinned me by the throat up against a wall and nearly blew my eyebrows off with his venom. 'You were with him! What happened? What happened?'

'He just got shot!' I yelled. 'We went through the fucking door and he went first and he got blasted!'

'And you didn't! You bloody didn't!'

God, if I'm not careful he's going to knife me! 'Because the guy's gun jammed and he dived out of the bloody window! It's not my fault, one of the guys in the street should have got him, what the hell were they out there for?'

Marko glared at me for a moment then spun away and picked on someone else. 'You were there! Why didn't you fuckin' get 'im!'

'I didn't bloody see anybody!'

Marko clubbed him in the teeth with his pistol. 'What, you fuckin' blind or somethink? You got no bleedin' eyes?' He started pistol-whipping the guy. 'You fuckin' let him get away you bastard!' The rest of us just stood watching.

I didn't feel too guilty about it. It was the guy who pissed on me. After a minute I looked away. But Marko didn't, he went on, on and on for about five minutes until his hand was raw and there was nothing left for him to smash. And then he stopped. I guess there's not so much fun in beating a corpse.

It wasn't a great day in the history of the Crucifixion Squad. I guess that's what it's like when you're on the decline. It was a bomb from start to finish.

C'est la vie I guess. I wouldn't be losing any sleep over it. I'd made up my mind, I was going to leave tonight. As soon as it was quiet. I should have gone last night. To hell with Homer. This is too much like suicide.

I looked down at my new jeans streaked with sewage, still dripping. Flies were crawling all over them. I'd have to burn them. What a bloody . . . Some days, it's just best not to get up at all. . . .

TWENTY

But it wasn't over. When it came to trouble, the day had hardly begun.

We straggled back to the tunnels beneath Junk City. A sorry bunch, sick on the taste of adventure gone wrong. The weapons weren't concealed now, they just dangled from weary fingers. We looked like the losers in a scrap. We were. And we were the only ones who'd bothered to turn up!

We picked our way through the rubbish, drifted down the ramp to the fly-bothered gloom of the main hall. As usual I was bringing up the rear.

Most of the squad had disappeared inside when there was an almighty bloody explosion and those of us still wandering in were blasted off our feet. A bomb had gone off in the tunnels.

The whumph! of the concussion wave left us numbed and deaf. We picked ourselves up, clawing off the dust and rubbish that had collapsed on us. My eyes were full of grit, I ground my thumbs in until they dripped. I couldn't stop coughing, all the oxygen seemed to have been sucked out of the air.

I staggered down the slope into the darkness. There were bodies everywhere. Some were still intact, others had taken refuge, in a dozen different places. There was a headless corpse at my feet and it was hardly bleeding, as though the blast had sealed all the vessels. And the spine had been severed as cleanly and neatly as if done on a butcher's block. I pulled it aside. It began to bleed then, pumping the stuff out.

I couldn't go any further. I could hear all the groaning and wailing, I could smell the burnt flesh. I didn't want to face that. And they were nothing to me. Couldn't see anything anyway for smoke and dust.

But some guys ran in – came out puking, smeared with blood. 'Get the doctors! For chrissake get the medics!'

'What doctors?' I said. 'What medics?'

'A cholera team came in last week,' someone said. It was Cheryl, cradling a broken arm. 'They're in one of the dumps!'

She set off up the slope, stumbling and sobbing. A cholera team? Maybe Sebastian was there. I ran on ahead, jumping over all the twisted metal. 'Where are they? Which one?'

'I don't know,' she said. She looked like she'd been beaten up as well, her face was bruised with shock and fright. She was blotched with blood. I think she was about to faint.

I sprinted across an open space as fast as I could go. Then I skidded to a halt, gawping.

Jesus H.!

About a hundred yards away, cresting a hump in the ground like a bunch of bloody Apaches, came a line of slewing motorcycles roaring like banshees! It was Angel's squad, you could tell them by the banner they carried – white wings on a black background. The Angels of Death!

They gunned the machines towards us. There must have been about thirty of them. And they started firing even as they bounced and screamed down the incline, even before they could see the whites of our faces. Holy gutted mackerel!

I turned round and ran. To hell with Cheryl, I left her floundering with her twisted arm and I went like a goddamn whippet.

It's funny the things that flash through your mind. You'd think the first thought would have been holy terror. I suppose it was really. But I also thought – where the hell did they get the petrol from? It's not a line of thought you can pursue far at a time like that though. I had enough to do keeping upright and keeping ahead.

The bikes howled, careering, leaping across the treacherous ground. They fanned out. In the silence of the day they split the ears.

Everyone in Marko's squad was dead. I realized that as I crashed down the slope to the survivors. They were going to be shot to pieces. They couldn't last five minutes. What the hell was I doing there?

As soon as I savvied that I veered off. I'd send in my formal resignation another time. I scrambled over a ridge of glass and cans. God, they'd fanned out so much they were in front of me again. Looked like they had shotguns.

I scampered off at a tangent, keeping low. I don't know where I was headed, but it was better than standing still. First rule of cowardice: always run.

But someone was ahead of me, sprinting across the ground. Christ, I'd have to tackle this one, he was right in front of me. I pulled up, spread my feet, took a two-handed grip. Take your time, I thought – don't be rushed, can't afford to miss. The sight moved on to him, finger tightened. It was David.

He rushed up to me, dragged me to the ground. 'Don't stand there like a prick!'

'Where've you been?'

'I've been looking for you the last few days. Shut up and listen – I found Homer!'

'What?'

'I shot him!'

'Shot him? When? Is he dead?'

'No, just now! A couple of minutes ago! Just before those bloody motorbikes appeared! He was headed this way! Didn't you see him?'

I shook my head. We flattened ourselves as a hail of pellets splatted into the garbage around us. David rolled over, let off four shots and the two guys on one of the bikes jerked off. He does everything so casually, like he hardly notices. It makes you sick!

'Who the hell are these guys?'

'One of the squads. Angel's mob. It's a takeover bid.'

'Where the hell has Homer got to though?' David got up on hands and knees. 'We'll try over that way. Come on.'

'Where did you shoot him? How bad is he?'

'I got him in the back. I should have dropped him.'

'How did you find him though?'

'I didn't, he just appeared. He was heading over this way.'

'Did he see you?'

'I don't know. I was about eighty yards away, on one of the towers.'

'You shot him from eighty yards – with a revolver?' I'd be lucky to hit him if he was standing at the end of the barrel.

'I rested on something. Come on.'

Christ, it could be nearly over. I checked my gun as I

ran, fired a shot at one of the Angels just to be sure. Missed of course. But my mind was on something else now. Homer. We had him as close as a gunshot. If we let him get away now, we probably wouldn't live to regret it.

But where was the bastard?

We dodged the bullets of the attacking squad of Angels. Just for a few moments my anxiety to finish Homer made me reckless of my safety. Ordinarily I'd have been digging a damn great burrow and waving a white flag. As it was, most of the attention was focused on the main hideout, where Marko's boys were making a desperate stand for survival. A desperate and futile stand. Their lives could be numbered in minutes.

Ours too maybe, if Homer wasn't too badly hurt. And he'd certainly managed to lose David, despite his wound.

We rounded a spur in this weird metal landscape – and there he was. He was limping but moving fast. As powerful and potent as the last time I'd seen him. Tall, heavy, seemingly oblivious to the world around. His head was still shaved, his skin still as white as if we'd just come through a winter. He had a light blue windcheater on, dark trousers, running shoes. He was carrying a pistol. And spreading from a mesial dark ring just below the ribs the blue of the jacket was turning red. He was maybe a hundred yards away by the time we negotiated a cobweb of barbed wire, crossing one of the few tarmac roads which traverse the area.

But he didn't cross it. He stopped at the verge, pulled up a metal grating, a drain or something. It must have weighed a ton, it clanged on the ground like a hammer on a ship. And he'd only used one hand to lift it. He should go in for arm wrestling.

As we started down the slight, grassy incline towards him he sat on the edge of the hole, slid out of sight. He hadn't seen us. Or had he? He looked back at the last moment. We put on a spurt. I had the terrible feeling that we might have just lost him.

I tripped over a tangle of rope. But even a twisted ankle wasn't going to stop me. I hobbled on grimly. That bastard Homer! Getting away! Right under our goddamn noses! Grrr!

We reached the hole. A square hatchway. We could hear water trickling below. Not another sewer is it? No, it's a river. Well, a stream at least. Stick your head over the edge David, see if he blows it off.

What to do? You can't just jump into a hole when you don't know what's waiting there.

David's a genius. While I'm debating he rips the rearview mirror from a Datsun, wraps it to a pole with a piece of wire. He lays flat, examines the interior like a dentist checking out a cavity in a leviathan. God, if only I had brains like that. 'What can you see?'

'Bugger all,' he muttered. 'Stupid bloody idea, I can't see a damn thing.' Homer might not realize that though. He wriggled forward, lowered his head gingerly over the edge.

'Can you see him?'

He shook his head. 'I can hear him. He's headed that way.' What way? He swung cautiously over the lip. 'Come on.' He vanished.

Blessed Mary, mother of God. . . . I followed.

It was a drop of a few feet, into shallow water. Only a few inches deep. It was like a long culvert, an adit maybe. Kind of roughly covered with stone. You could just walk without stooping. It was about seven, eight feet wide. It must take the stream to the Thames – how far is that, a mile, mile and a half? Something like that.

It was an ambivalent place, buzzing with tension yet strangely peaceful; not like the rank, sordid world of the sewers. Here you could see a way because of the gratings that were situated at odd intervals. But it was shadowy. Some stretches were more tenebrous than you'd like. We set off in pursuit of the lethal albino, sliding and stumbling like drunks on the backs of the round, mossy stones that lay under the water.

We went a couple of hundred yards, squinting into the beckoning gloom. Once or twice we heard splashes. But we saw nothing. Just a few rats. We hadn't spoken. We were too busy listening.

We saw the flash of Homer's gun an instant before hearing it. We flung ourselves against the walls as a bullet passed between us, went pinging down the tunnel, ricocheting off the walls. I clung on like a parasite in someone's gut. After a minute David nudged me, whispered me on.

We kept as far apart as we could. It was no good just blasting into the murk ahead, he'd drop us sure as eggs is eggs. We had to get the bastard in our sights. I started wheezing. It must be a nervous reaction. I had to keep crouching down while I cleared mucus from my throat. Must see a doc, if I survive.

Ten minutes passed. And again. We came to a fork in the tunnel. The river continued to the left. To the right was a dry bed. Which way would he go? We crouched, straining. Nothing. The minutes ticked by. Or would have done if we'd had a watch. A tiny splash. A rat maybe? David touched my arm. We followed the river. We crouched even lower. We felt close.

The tunnel took a wide turn. We'd been down there for about half an hour and it seemed like four lifetimes. The tension sure as hell wasn't getting any less. As the turn straightened grey evening light crept in, a hundred yards on. And just moving into it, a stooped figure. The albino!

All the tension suddenly snapped into the guns. We whipped them up together, fired at the same moment. Pow pow pow! Must have sent a dozen slugs winging down the tunnel. He vanished. We were nearly flaming deafened by the noise, my ears were clanging like bells. We began to run, splashing and tumbling, crashing on our knees. Stopped just long enough to reload.

We came out in the docks. Long abandoned. Small-time stuff anyway, just a few old, rotten, wooden wharves, a pair of deserted warehouses, wondering where their roofs had gone. We blinked in the steely light. God, we must be so close to him. . . . There was blood glistening on the slimy mud.

And then he was there! Right in front of us, about thirty yards away, standing on one of the wharves. His gun aimed right at us. We dived into the mud as bullets thwacked all about us. He ran to the end of the wharf – he was going to dive in! 'Get him!!' I blasted away for all I was worth, emptying the goddamn gun. There was a terrific splash.

We got him! We must have got him! Surely to God. . . .

We charged across a tract of gunge and mud, sliding on our bellies as we both tripped over a rope. Up a rotten wooden ladder on to the wharf, a warehouse looming on the right. We sprinted to the end. A bright patch of blood on the mossy timber. We trained our guns on the sluggish, flat waves of the river.

'Where is he?' I hissed. I wanted to shoot him. I wanted to shoot his goddamn head off.

'I don't know,' muttered David.

'Did we get him?'

He nodded. 'Yeah. We hit him half a dozen times. He was kicking like a puppet.'

The turgid brown water flowed enigmatically past. It looked like welfare canteen tea, right down to the flecks of foam. A tang of smoke sought us out. A breeze pushed upriver, licked our faces, just tasting us. It flickered our collars. I shivered.

'He'd have had to come up for air. He must be dead. He's probably caught in the currents.'

And somehow then, I knew he was dead. Something in my belly told me. I waited another moment, then let my gun fall to my side. We'd killed him. We'd tracked him to the end. He should have won, but he hadn't. He'd turned his back to David, blown it. He'd missed us at the crucial moment. Maybe the pain unnerved him, I don't know. But we were alive, and he'd gone.

All those months of waiting. . . . Maybe it's just as well I didn't see his corpse. It's better that he's just gone, swept away like a sackful of dirt. I squatted down, put my gun on the deck. I had to prise my finger out of it, it had kind of locked with tension. My breath trembled as it went through my throat. I let out an enormous sigh.

At last I was able to speak. 'I never really thought we'd do it you know, Dave.'

He shook his head. I saw that he was trembling. That's the first time I've seen him do that. 'Somehow – it turned out easier than it should have been.' He didn't say any more.

Maybe at last our luck was changing. I sat down, my

feet dangling over the edge. We could still hear gunfire punching holes in the docklight stillness from the direction of Junk City. But that aside it was quiet. Peaceful as a photograph. We didn't have anything to do now. We could just sit there, and think, and maybe. . . .

A voice muttered right behind us. 'Leave the gun right there, cully. And you drop yours into the bloody river boy.'

It was Tommy. He brought ice with him, his words were glaciers, they cut into the depths of our guts.

I turned around numbly. Oh my Jesus Christ. He stepped out of the warehouse shadows. Oh God, I'd thought he was gone. I thought he was gone. I squeezed my eyes in a sudden desolation.

I heard David's pistol splash quiescently into the river. I stood up slowly.

Tommy approached, limping. He nodded at it as we both glanced down at his leg. 'Cut me fucking leg on a piece of glass an' all!' He halted maybe fifteen feet away, his machine gun pointing at our bellies like the penis of death. He rested it on his hip.

'So you got him then, cully? You got him – eh?' I nodded. I seemed to have no feelings left in me. It just – I don't know what to say really. I've had everything knocked out of me. I glance at David. He looks as stunned as me. His lips are white.

'Quite a chase you had boys. Quite a chase. You deserved him.' He hawks, spits. He doesn't look too healthy, looks like he's been living rough. 'I've been staking this place out for a couple o' weeks now boy. I knew he'd come. You get a kind of – sixth sense, d'yez know what I mean? And sure enough, so he did 'n all. And there was yon pretty boy, plugging holes in his back, from miles an' miles away.' He shakes his head.

220

'Jeez, that's a hell of a gun hand you've got there!' He becomes quiet, thinking of something that's probably not important. He looks away into the distance.

'You don't have to kill us Tommy.'

He hawks again. He must have bronchitis or something. 'Oh I do, boyo. Begod I do. Aye, and you thought you'd bloody won eh? You thought you'd bloody won.' He shakes his head. His eyes suddenly freeze. 'No cully, yez haven't won. Yez haven't won at all.' He looks right at me. 'Yez haven't won a fuckin' thing. . . .' His voice fades away.

My stomach lurches as the gun levels in his hands and he braces his feet. I shut my eyes as the barrel swings on to me. I turn towards David. Oh God, God, he's going to murder us!

I scream.

And the gun roars. De-De-De-De-De! I slump to my knees with a thud, choking, gagging.

But it wasn't me who died. The bullet holes tearing through my chest didn't come. The longest scream wasn't mine. Well, the longest was; the loudest too. But not the most surprised.

The clatter of death didn't come from Tommy's gun. It came from somewhere to the left, spitting out of the warehouse shadows. I looked up through a haze, in time to see the little Irishman sag at the knees, twist to the floor mewling.

His side and his arm were full of holes. The arm was hanging off, there was only a piece of tattered muscle holding it on, and that was tearing as he struggled on the ground like a winged bird.

'Do you want to kill him?' It was a woman's voice. I

squinted into the dimness, looking for her. She stepped towards us. It was Marsha.

I didn't say anything. I just looked at her, gulping, snorting.

She stood over Tommy, waited until he turned his head to look at her, blasted it to mincemeat. He was only a tiny guy, he looked like a boy huddled there in death. He looked like a little boy, whose head had been hit by a train.

A bike snarled up, skidded to a halt, hung there like a dog. Marsha made a face at me, slung the gun across her back, climbed aboard. They went without a word.

A silence descended on us.

For a couple of minutes I just knelt there staring into space, calming down, trying to figure out how much it finally takes to club your sanity out of you. I let the knots in my belly try to unravel themselves but they didn't find it easy. I didn't even have it in me to wipe the saliva that I'd dribbled on to my chin. The last few minutes were like – like they couldn't have really happened.

Finally David shuffled and spoke. 'Would you mind telling me what the hell all that was about?' He didn't find it easy to speak either. His voice was husky.

I shook my head. The best I could do was shrug. 'It must have been my fairy godmother.'

And all of a sudden, I felt – numb. Two of my enemies, Homer and Tommy, were dead. Marko's squad was smashed. In the space of a few minutes the world had become a lot quieter. Funny how quickly the fear subsides.

It was like the closing of a chapter. A series of bizarre adventures, culminating in the deaths on this lonely wharf. The quick exchange of victory, dismay, disbelief, relief. For the first time in a couple of years I didn't have to worry about who was lurking around the next corner. Well, maybe not quite so much as usual.

It was a little, I don't know, unsettling in a way. I'm used to having something to worry about. I mean, I was relieved it was all over. But now something else had to begin. Where do we go, David and I, from here? We'd won a battle, but what about the war? We're still wanted by the police; the army's still got me on its books. Is there another battlefield, another arena waiting? I don't know. I don't know why I bother asking these questions really, I never get anywhere.

All I do know is, we've got to push on. Every day we hesitate, America drifts a little further away, Harry and Rachel get a little bit harder to find. It's no good hoping time is going to sort things out for you.

I lifted my eyes to the yawning shades, the tarnished lead of an autumn sky. The air was bruising with darkness. The hour of lamps. I looked up at David. 'Where do we go now?'

He crouched down beside me, shook us out a couple of ciggies, lit them pensively. He sighed through his nostrils, let uninhaled smoke curl from his mouth, watched it jerk away on the anabatic evening air. 'We could go and get a cup of tea,' he said.

Yeah, right. Turning, as I pushed myself up, I caught a movement in the shadows at the farther end of the warehouse.

What was that, a kid or what? God, I hope it was a kid. Because if it wasn't, it must have been a bloody dwarf. Two of them there were, in that photograph in the dead dwarf's pocket.

And I have a ghastly feeling we've just seen the second one.

THE MASQUERS

Natasha Peters

For the wealthy, life in eighteenth-century Venice is a never-ending carnival, teeming with mystery and immorality. Gondolas glide soundlessly through narrow canals, carrying masked lovers to secret trysts. It is a city of intrigue, of beauty and of exquisite sensuality . . . and Fosca Loredan is a woman of Venice.

Magnificently beautiful, wildly passionate, Fosca Loredan has bewitched three demanding lovers: Alessandro, her older, aristocratic husband; Raf Leopardi, bold revolutionary and her husband's deadliest enemy; and Venice itself, a lover who insists that her people conform or be banished from the palaces of pleasure.

Fosca must choose, for she cannot have them all.